QUEEN'S CROWN

CROWNKEEPER BOOK THREE

ANNE WHEELER

narcienne
crasquet river
tourmel mountains
Mencote Desert
kalcine river
bran
winson lake
edris
Coalwood Basin
bolcour mountains
n
w
e
s
inn
heosta

THE KINGDOM OF
MEIRDRE
t river
vistel
arsele forest
lochfield castle
szen
elternow
the moors
harnow
Galvan Ocean
utpost
windersay

PROLOGUE

LAURENT

MEIRDRE HAD ENDURED WAR BEFORE, BUT Laurent was too young to know it. So too had been his father and grandfather. The stories of battles and bodies and sobbing women? They haunted him, yes, but that was all they were to him—stories from decades upon decades ago, before he had so much as existed.

Yes, wars were bedtime tales like the ones his nurse had tried to frighten him with as soon as she'd deemed him an appropriate age to hear. Or fiction, like the myths of dragons roaming his kingdom, long before such accounts were written. Legend had it, at least among his ancestors, that the enchanted map in the ballroom of Lochfeld Castle had been created in a desperate attempt to protect Meirdre from the winged beasts which had once turned the countryside to ashes every few years. That wasn't true—the timeline didn't even make sense—but no one could blame the royal family for coming up with such a story. Even magic could be turned into something mundane when ignored for so many years, and Riette was the first Meirdrean crownkeeper in a long while.

And now, as he'd told her last night, the dragons were coming again. Flesh and bone humans they might be, but did that matter in the end? The Kingdom of Vassian could do as much damage as a pair of dragons. Maybe more, for even dragons satiated themselves eventually, a constraint to which the Vassian king—Damir—didn't seem willing to subject himself.

Laurent glanced behind him, at the soldiers breaking camp in the meadow outside Lochfeld. They weren't ready for all-out war, having spent his entire reign patrolling the kingdom, running off pirates, protecting the borders. Dew lingered on the grass as the soldiers prowled about, and his fingers cramped in the chill as he fastened his scabbard around his belt and slid his sword inside. He'd spent the night here on the hard ground with the soldiers who would ride off to the Vassian border, loyal to their own deaths.

Well, most of the night.

The scent of Riette's rose perfume clung to his shirt, and he hadn't the heart to exchange it for a clean one. No one said anything within ear shot about the king wearing a dirty shirt that smelled of his wife, though had Willem been here, he'd have subjected him to a good-natured jibe—but naturally, if Willem had been here, there'd be no cause to ride to war. Not as much cause, at least.

The camp grew louder as he wandered to the edge and stared south, past the castle. Laurent wanted to draw the sword and practice, but that might show fear, anxiety, apprehension—and that, he would never do. Not even when his soldiers were preoccupied with wagons and stallions and muskets and tents.

He went through a few motions in his head, deliberately not looking up toward the windows of the sprawling fortress in front of him. Riette would be watching, and if he saw her, he might lose his nerve, run back inside the castle, sweep her into his arms, carry her back to his bed . . .

No. He'd never abandon his duty to Meirdre and Riette herself, even if his very soul cried out for her and whatever magic she'd bewitched him with. When—*if*—he came home, he'd do that. But if he thought about that now, he would keep thinking of her instead of keeping his mind on strategy, and he would not betray his duty.

Someone hollered behind him, and he turned to see one of the captains hurrying toward him, Foxfire's reins in his hand. The stallion was fairly glistening with the shine of a recent brushing—that was Riette's doing as well—but he was nervous, that much was clear in his sidestep and the way he tossed his head upon seeing his master.

Skidding to a halt, the captain said, "They're ready, Your Majesty." He gave a brief bow, but it was difficult to tell if he or the horse was more anxious. "Waiting on your word."

Laurent nodded. "Cadaval, is it?"

"Yes, sire. Third Company. Out of Brannitz."

Their route to the Vassian border would

take them straight through there—for a night only. "Going home, then."

"Passing through, sire, yes." Firefox reared, and Cadaval gripped the reins harder, then lifted them in an offering—or perhaps a plea. The stallion had that effect on people. "He wants to run."

Foxfire always did. Laurent patted him on the flank, then turned back to Cadaval.

"I need someone at my side," he said. "But I will not order it of you."

Not after what happened before.

Cadaval lowered his head. "I would be honored, sire."

"So quickly you agree." His brows rose. Impetuousness from a senior leader would not serve him well. "You're not aware of what happened to your predecessor, then?"

Laurent still had nightmares about Willem's headless body lying in front of the throne inside Lochfeld. The blood, the violation of someone not only entering the castle, but taking his most trusted guard's life. Did a man ever forget something like that? He wasn't sure he could. Or should.

Cadaval's stance grew straighter and, if possible, more sober. "I am."

Laurent focused on the ground, as if it could suggest a suitable reply for him.

"Well." Shouldn't ordering a loyal man to almost certain death make him *feel* something more? Instead, he only wanted everything over with, however it was to end. Like Foxfire, he was suddenly ready to be underway. "Then let's be off, shall we? Inform the men."

Cadaval saluted him before departing. The gesture made Laurent strangely uncomfortable after his more informal relationship with Willem, but the captain would learn what it meant to serve him—if he survived long enough.

"Sire!"

Laurent twisted around at Father Gerritt's voice and forced a half-smile. He'd spent the morning avoiding the priest and his bottle of oil, convinced of the futility of its meaning. Besides, didn't accepting last rites, as many of the soldiers had, imply certain defeat? He wasn't an optimist, especially now, but there was certainty, and then there was *certainty*.

"You found me at last, Father." He raised his arms to his sides in surrender. "Congratulations."

"So I did." Gerritt's lips twisted in amusement. "Much as you've been attempting to dodge me all morning."

"I've been busy. So much to do. You know that." The reply was too short, and his shoulders sagged. Gerritt wasn't someone he could brush off—ever. "But I am glad to see you before we leave."

"As am I—and never fear, I won't subject you to any long lectures about war and death and life."

Laurent burst into laughter, something he'd only ever done among a handful of men. Still, it must be anxiety now. Who laughed before riding off for war?

"No? Then I *am* curious about what's so important for you to spend hours tracking me down, Father."

"Riette."

"Ah." Her very name pierced his heart. "Riette. How is she?"

"Holding up. She knows her duty, and she'll fulfill it if it's the last thing she does."

"Good," Laurent breathed out. He wanted happiness for her, but duty would have to do for now. "Good."

"But what she doesn't know," Gerritt went on casually, "and what I suspect you're not aware of either, is that more magic than the map enchants Meirdre. All related, of course."

Laurent glanced to the side, at the soldiers and horses surrounding them, certain he'd misheard given the din of a departing military camp. He'd had wine last night, yes, but ... *more magic?*

"I'm—I'm sorry?" Confusion laced his words. "I don't understand."

Gerritt folded his arms and smiled, smug as always. "Because you rarely accept my offers to explore Lochfeld's library, sire."

Irritation swelled over the confusion. "Yes, yes. I neglected my education, but it's a bit late to be lecturing me about that now. Speak and speak quickly."

So Gerritt did, and Laurent listened. And when the priest was done, Laurent let him apply the oil before saying goodbye, even though it seemed more meaningless now than before. Heaving himself up upon Foxfire, he dug in his heels and focused on the trail in front of him, ignoring how Lochfeld was fading in the distance behind him, Riette along with it.

The future of Meirdre was in his hands now.

The future of Lochfeld?

In Riette's.

On second thought, he realized, as the trail descended the cliff and Foxfire's stride grew more intentional . . .

Maybe Riette would save both.

CHAPTER ONE

Hooves thundered as I stared out the window. There was no dust, thanks to last night's rain, only a field of mud where short, spring grass had grown only ten days before. It would harden soon enough—that much I knew from the sun that warmed my face and mocked the chill in the rest of my body. Laurent was gone, and heavens, but I wanted his arms around me still.

Bottles rattled behind me. Sara was arranging the things on top of my chest, not-so-surreptitiously waiting for me to choose a gown for the day. I needed to, since the map was waiting, but pretty fabric seemed frivolous. As frivolous as I'd thought it when I had first come to Lochfeld.

Then again, I realized, as I shook off the memory of Laurent's arms, Lochfeld was mine to care for now, and that meant acting the part. Servants and soldiers who prowled the corridors—they needed that from me as well, didn't they? I truly had no idea. I was wholly unprepared for this kind of responsibility.

A bottle crashed to the floor, and I turned.

"I'm so sorry, Your Grace." Sara knelt to gather the shards, but I waved her off.

"Leave it." I sighed and picked at the skirt of my nightclothes. "You're right—I need to get dressed."

Sara sprang to her feet all too willingly and yanked a deep blue gown from my wardrobe. Feigning interest and marveling at how she could pretend today was just another day, I raised my arms over my head and allowed her to dress me. Maybe pretending was the only thing that kept her sane. If that was the case, I could do it as well.

I kept pretending as I wandered downstairs toward the ballroom, footsteps of strangers behind me. The royal guard had always been uninvolved in my security by my request. But Laurent had ordered both them and the soldiers to keep a close watch on me after he departed, and so far, they'd listened. That would have to change—it was already suffocating—but for now I'd pretend that didn't bother me, either.

Shadows crumpled in the corners as a servant lit the oil lamps behind me. Light didn't matter since I could read the map in pitch blackness, but I suspected they thought I was addled enough as it was, so I didn't argue. The provisional mistress of Lochfeld couldn't be seen sitting alone in a dark room. That was how rumors began and reigns ended, however temporary both might be.

I sat by the narrow window, letting the sliver of light from outside try to warm me once more. Normally I practiced a waltz, a minuet, or even one of the Elternow folk dances I'd learned in childhood, but I'd already used up my desire for subterfuge in simply getting dressed.

Heavens, Laurent would be aghast by my moping if he could see me now.

Grumbling to myself, I stood and circled the map inlaid on the floor. Harnow, thankfully, was quiet. So too was Lochfeld, Elternow, and the Vassian border. That was something, at least. Though Laurent was confident of the tiny Meirdrean army's ability to defend the kingdom, they were spread much too thin already. Would I be able to order the soldiers who remained at Lochfeld away if they became needed elsewhere? The woman who Laurent had trusted with his castle said yes. The terrified child in me said no.

Then again, as Lieutenant Julian Vahl cleared his throat behind me, I decided that war might be worth it if only to force him to leave Lochfeld for good. I pinned on a smile before greeting the one person who still seemed to doubt my innocence in this entire mess.

"Good morning, Lieutenant. Come to make certain I haven't absconded with yet another traitor?"

Vahl folded his hands behind his back. "They sent me to fetch you. For a meeting."

"They? A meeting?" My forehead creased.

He gestured out the door with his chin, and I followed beside him through hallways that were too quiet for late morning. Lochfeld was quiet on the best of the days, what with Laurent's lack of a full court, but there was something about her sovereign being gone that gave an eerie ambience to the place that had finally become my home.

By the time Vahl ushered me into the war room, my mind was racing with possibilities. Part of my soul wondered if Laurent was inside, but that was foolish, and if I'd learned anything since he'd ridden off for the Vassian border earlier this morning, it was that fool hope was the last refuge of . . . well, fools. The Riette who'd left Elternow on that snowy winter's night believed in such things. The Riette who stepped inside the octagonal chamber did not.

Every oil lamp was lit, casting sharp shadows on the center table and the tiny soldiers standing there. Most had been moved south, toward Vassian, leaving a single figure remaining on top of Lochfeld and a few others scattered toward the north. I wanted to rearrange them, to move several of the southern ones back up to where I stood, but I steadied myself and looked toward the highest-ranking man in the room, a captain in a pristine uniform like Vahl's but with the tall boots of a cavalry officer.

"Yes?" I asked, leveling my shoulders and attempting to fake a modicum of authority. "Has something happened?"

Has something happened?

How naïve could I sound? Laurent had just left. Of course nothing had happened.

"No, Your Grace." The captain bowed quickly, then meandered around the table toward me. "Tobias Erstad. I only wanted to introduce myself and fill you in on the plans for protecting Lochfeld."

I took a breath. Laurent had said as much, and I'd been ready to fulfill the duties his departure had imposed upon me. But hearing it now, like this . . . that was a reminder that I wasn't ready for.

Still, I nodded. "Which are?"

Erstad elaborated as he pointed at the map every so often and asked for clarification from one soldier or another in the room. I tried to keep up with his explanation, which I suspected he was simplifying for my benefit, but the only strategy I understood was leaving a cadre of soldiers here to patrol. I couldn't argue against that, as much as I hated the castle being turned into a place of war.

Biting the inside of my cheek, I glanced at the thick stone wall next to me. Lochfeld had *always* been a place of war, splintered by slender arrows of peace. When would I learn? Never, it seemed.

"And Laur—the king?"

"It's several weeks to the Illrus River." Erstad pointed casually, not calling attention to my lack of geographical awareness. "Scouts are following behind, but I wouldn't expect any kind of news for a long while."

"So we are safe at Lochfeld."

"For now," he replied.

For now.

The stone walls seemed to cave in around me, and I sucked in a breath.

"And Lochfeld is . . ." What was that word he'd used? "Defensible? We are prepared for a long siege?"

Food, water, medicinal supplies—I ran through a list in my head. If Laurent hadn't stored enough in the castle, I wasn't sure what I would do. Taking more from the subjects around Lochfeld would be impossible.

"Without a doubt, Your Grace. It's stood through worse than the Kingdom of Vassian can bring."

Laurent hadn't sounded so certain, and I knew Erstad was afraid I'd panic if he told me the truth. I nodded again, like I'd probably done throughout his entire update.

"All right, then." I bit my lip. "And how long until—until we can expect something to happen here?"

He shrugged. "Weeks, certainly. If there's anywhere you want to visit, anyone you need to see beforehand . . . you'd best do it soon. Even if you only want to explore the countryside."

I pressed my lips together. Explore the countryside? Didn't he know I couldn't leave Lochfeld?

But Queen Silke had.

Somehow, she had. She'd found a way to travel the kingdom and still watch the map. Free from Lochfeld, she'd still been able to protect Meirdre. I just needed to figure out how.

And even if I couldn't . . . if war was coming, I knew exactly where I needed to go first.

CHAPTER TWO

MOONLIGHT GLISTENED OVER THE MOORS, casting shadows across the rolling hills. Below us, in what passed for a valley, Elternow sat, scarcely more than a cluster of homes. I hadn't seen it in months, and then it had been covered in snow. Tonight, though, the spring breeze whipped my loose hair about me as I urged Skylark closer.

It hadn't been my idea, not exactly. Well, riding all this way had—though a carriage followed with my things, doubling as shelter during the night. Laurent would be furious if he knew I'd left Lochfeld, and to tell the truth, I was already second-guessing my decision. But the map had been clear that no harm would befall Meirdre soon.

At least from the south, from Vassian's army. The rest? I hated to admit I didn't know.

"It's hardly even a village." Erstad edged beside me on his horse as we headed down the hill. "Do you miss it?"

"There's hardly anything to miss." I stared off into the distance, searching for Mama and Papa's house. The lights were too difficult to see from all this way, so I turned my attention back to him. "Just some horses and small homes."

And Mama, Papa, apple trees, clean snow in the winter, the bright smell of a new calf in spring, and . . .

Even that crack in the window of the cottage where I'd grown up.

Well, what did it matter? I was only visiting one last time, then I would head back to Lochfeld and whatever disaster the future held for it. Once I returned to the castle and the two fireplaces that had kept my room warm for the remainder of last winter, I would laugh at the fact I'd missed that drafty room where the royal guard had stood that night. It seemed like so long ago.

"And hay, it appears." Erstad pointed toward town, toward a stack in the distance. "Odd it's sitting out right now."

Odd indeed. Even the poorest farmers in Elternow had shared barns for wintering their crops. Feeding the livestock was just that important where I'd grown up. And for it to be left in the fields . . .

Soldiers burned them. Thomas's voice echoed in my mind, as clearly as it had when we'd played as children, when Laurent had condemned us both to death. *As they were stacked.*

Ice slunk down my spine. Soldiers, like

the man who rode with me now? Like the four others trailing behind us? Had I allowed myself to be escorted by criminals?

Silly.

I hadn't been afraid of Captain Erstad back at Lochfeld, and Laurent had trusted him enough to leave him in charge of the castle's security—and mine. But Thomas's claim was so hard to dismiss, though I'd tried as we'd ridden through the fields west of the Arsele, but he'd slammed me down. It was arson, and the Meirdrean Army was responsible, he'd insisted. Wouldn't hear anything else about it.

But now . . . now Thomas had proven himself a traitor by selling Laurent and Meirdre out to Vassian. By using me, heedless of the fact it had almost cost me my life in the Lochfeld's dungeon. By murdering Willem in Lochfeld itself. He wasn't just a rebel anymore, for I could understand that kind of motivation. I didn't agree with it, now that I knew *why* Laurent's coffers were in the shape they were in, but I could understand it.

But murder? And the things he'd done to me?

Maybe Thomas was wrong about the destruction of the haystacks, too. Erstad had commented on them, after all. He wouldn't have called attention to them if the army had been responsible.

I sighed and tightened my grip on Skylark's reins.

"It's just mold," I replied. "Life is hard in Elternow."

Candlelight flickered in that cracked window as I pulled Skylark to a stop outside Mama and Papa's house. Late it might be, but surely she was still working on her mending. It wouldn't be Papa, since I could see two figures moving around inside the open barn, the hired boy that Laurent's money allowed for, along with Papa himself. Most of me wondered why he was working at all—his fingers were much too twisted with gout to handle that kind of labor, but that was Papa. *Roland is help*, his last letter had said. *Not someone to do everything for me.*

The door opened as I tossed the reins over Skylark's back and let one of the soldiers lead her toward the barn. Mama stuck her head outside, and I flew to her, burying my head on her shoulder.

"Riette, what in the heavens are you doing here?"

She patted my head, and through my emotion, I realized she was concerned. How had I not appreciated how my arrival would look to her?

"Just visiting. I missed you, and—" I pried myself away and forced a weary smile. Laurent hadn't specifically said not to talk about it, and although I was sure rumors of the army headed south had made it to Elternow, somehow speaking of war now seemed wrong. "It was the right time."

"But on a horse! Riette!"

"There's a carriage trailing us." I waved behind me, though I doubted she could see it in the dark. "I wanted to ride—and when you meet Skylark, you'll understand why."

"Well—" Her hands fluttered in front of her. "Come in, then. There's not much to eat, not prepared at least, but perhaps I can find something."

Before I could protest that we'd brought our own food, she darted inside, her mumblings trailing away. I followed her, wordless. Perhaps she didn't want more charity. Erstad had disappeared with his own horse, but I thought I heard his voice somewhere out toward the barn. For a moment, I thought about going out and rescuing Papa from that awkward introduction, but when Mama placed a hot cup of apple water in my hands, I stopped.

"This smells wonderful." I greedily inhaled the scent of my childhood. Too poor for actual tea back then, dried bits of apple in water had made an acceptable substitute—or so I'd thought before I'd known better. Still, it was comforting. "But you didn't have to waste your provisions on me."

"Nonsense." Mama settled into her chair, her eyes glinting with some sort of joke. "I'm saving the tea you sent for myself."

I burst into laughter as I sat across from her, spilling some of the water across my wrist. "I'm glad. And even gladder Papa seems healthier. That's him in the barn, isn't it?"

"It is." She nodded. "He rubs that medication into his hands every morning, and—Riette, you wouldn't believe the change in him. It's an absolute miracle. And if you hadn't—"

"I was happy to do it," I whispered. I

hadn't been that night, but what other option had I had? Leave them to poverty when I'd had a chance to save them?

Mama leaned forward. "But are you happy now?"

I raised the cup to my lips, wished it was Laurent's lips instead, then lowered it.

"I was. But now he's gone, and I—" *Stupid tears.* "Some—some things have happened. I was happy. And now I'm not."

"We heard of the army headed toward the Vassian border," Mama replied. "He was leading them?"

I nodded, miserably.

"And you love him?"

Again, I nodded. It felt like I was confessing to a crime.

"Well—" Her expression grew comforting. "I suppose I see why you're here now. How long do you intend to stay?"

I clutched at the apple water. The map hadn't called to me like it had when I'd been visiting Laurent's mother in Iraela, but that didn't mean it was completely quiet. Did it? Or was that how Silke reined in its power? Did she simply rush home when it bid her to? That seemed too simple.

"Not long," I replied. "Likely just long enough to recover from the trip. While the king is away, Lochfeld is my responsibility, and..."

"I understand." Her smile grew tight, as if she'd realized my position, windfall as it was to her and Papa, had put me in danger. "Then we'll enjoy every minute we have together, won't we?"

I nodded as the door swung open again.

"Nice horse you have," Papa's voice boomed. He shoved his hands in his pockets before I could confirm what Mama had said about his fingers.

He hadn't sounded that strong in years, and I sprang from my chair to embrace him.

He smelled like horse and sweat, but then again, so did I.

"She's lovely, Papa." He'd never been given much to emotion, so horse talk it was. "And she's taught me brilliantly."

"Nice horses the soldiers have, too."

I sighed and backed away.

"Yes—well. I'm sure you've heard about the attack on Lochfeld. What's left of the royal guard must stay with the king. He spared a few soldiers to protect Lochfeld."

Wherever he is.

"And its queen?"

"Well, yes. Me, too."

Papa made an ambiguous sound in his throat.

"At least they brought their own hay," he replied. "Since they destroyed the rest, we're a little scarce on feed."

Not this again. But Papa, at least, was more trustworthy than Thomas. Maybe I could get an answer out of him.

"How did they do that?"

"It molded."

"Not burned?"

He laughed, though it didn't sound humorous. "The stacks are still standing, aren't they? If you burn them, they'd be nothing more than a flat pile of burned grass on the ground. Transfer mold spores from somewhere else, though, and add some water—you've just destroyed any chance a farmer has at feeding his livestock in the winter."

"But—" I slammed my mouth closed. Thomas *had* lied, and I felt like an idiot for believing him.

"Ah, it doesn't matter." Papa waved a hand toward the fields. "If they try anything again, we'll know just who did it. And they won't get away with it this time."

CHAPTER THREE

Mornings in Elternow were always cool in the spring, and as I dressed myself for the first time in months, I couldn't keep the haystacks out of my mind. All night I'd tossed and turned in my old bed, lumpy and creaky, wondering what motivation Thomas had for lying to me. Why had I fallen for it?

At heart, I was a peasant girl, after all, though one who'd never seen a haystack torched, naturally. I grumbled at that as I pulled an untailored muslin gown over my head. How could I have been such a . . . girl? But to my relief, nothing more was said of the haystacks and soldiers when I stepped into the main room, and Mama simply smiled and handed me a cup of tea.

"From Brannitz," she said. "Can you believe it? They buy the tea from a plantation somewhere across the sea, then dry and make it in Meirdre. I never thought such a thing was possible."

It was something that was part of my life now, but I smiled as I took it. "You're sharing now, Mama—but you truly don't need to."

She pointed toward the cellar underneath the cottage. "They brought food. Unloaded it after you went to sleep. You must have been exhausted, because you slept through all the commotion."

I hadn't even realized I'd slept more than five minutes at a time last night, much less through soldiers tromping through the house. I gulped down some of the tea, glanced down the ladder into the shadows of the cellar, then hesitated.

"Papa is outside?"

"Feeding the cows. Roland wasn't feeling so well this morning. His sister sent word." Mama wiped her hands on her skirts. "I was just about to start breakfast for you and your escorts, but it appears they have their own food and no problems cooking it themselves. So—what would you like?"

"An apple?" I asked. Truthfully, I wasn't very hungry, and I wanted to explore, like I hadn't done much of at all since Laurent had departed. And gallivanting around Elternow on a warm spring day had a definite appeal.

"Only dried ones right now."

Mama pointed at the basket, and I grabbed a handful of slices, my mouth watering. Dried and a season old or not, I could hardly wait to shove them in my mouth.

With a wave, I headed out toward the barn, chomping on my breakfast, thankful, for the first time, that Laurent couldn't see me. I was still laughing at the way he would have looked at the way I was eating when Papa came out of the barn, hefting a bag of grain.

"Let me get that," I said, shoving the slices in my pocket and darting toward him. "You should have woken me up to help."

"Riette." His brows rose as he dropped the bag on the ground and eyed the brown damask I wore. "The king's wife, helping with livestock? What would people think?"

"Papa, I didn't come here to be waited on."

My hurt must have been obvious, for he sighed.

"I know you didn't. And yet—we're fine. Roland has been a great help to us, and I could have waited for his return, yes, but—"

"But you needed something to do."

"If you'd perhaps sent word—"

"Security." My response was clipped. "Even a letter might have been . . . unwise."

Papa exhaled again. "I understand."

"The bag?"

"Is too heavy for you to lift." He hefted it over his shoulder once more and tromped to the pen behind me. "Though I appreciate the offer."

I followed, my skirts trailing along in the dust. The pen was new since my departure, and when I looked inside, dark eyes over a pink snout stared back at me.

"You have a hog!" I said as the creature ambled toward me.

Papa dumped the feed to the ground once more and placed his hands on his hips. "She'll fill the cellar nicely next winter, won't she?"

"Indeed." I reached down and ran my fingers along the top of her head. "Or produce babies to fill the cellar later."

"Riette! For heaven's sake."

"You sound like Mama." I rolled my eyes and sidestepped a roaming chicken. "It's not as though I've never helped you deliver a calf."

"Well, that is accurate enough. But you're a different person now, and the king wouldn't approve of such talk." He stood there, regarding me. "Now off with you. I have work to do, and I assume you're not here to do farm chores."

I sighed. There was no arguing with Papa sometimes.

"Are the apple trees blooming yet?" I asked.

"In the Caballero's orchard." Papa pointed, then laughed. "But don't let the owners see you—unless you feel like playing their idea of a princess."

Hoary petals drifted through the air like silk as I strolled through the orchard edging the Caballero farm, smiling at Papa's warning. I'd wondered what the rest of Elternow thought of me since I'd left to marry Laurent, and now I knew—if only *they* knew how little I'd changed. Especially with the way I was eyeing the tree at the perimeter of the orchard, an enormous thing with gnarly, twisted branches that reached toward the sky.

The tree I'd used to sit in and watch for the king's men coming up the trail through the nearby thicket.

The bark was rough under my hand as I ran my palm down it, acutely aware of how the king's wife shouldn't be climbing trees. But I was also acutely aware that the orchard was empty. Even Captain Erstad was back at the barn doing whatever it was soldiers did in the mornings, which meant I was freer than I'd been in months.

With one last glance around, I placed my foot on the trunk and hoisted myself into the bottom cleft. The tree didn't so much as wobble under my weight, and I lifted my skirts around my knees to better climb to my former spot. Laurent would have a stroke if he could see me now.

But as Father Gerritt had once told him, I needed contact with the land for my gift to work, and he didn't just mean the ground itself. So I climbed upward, shaking apple blossoms from my hair and feeling for just the right handholds, until I reached that spot I'd loved so much. The ground was far below me, but the tree was sturdy enough that I had no fear of falling. Pale green leaves that were finally replacing the flowers concealed my presence, and I leaned against the trunk, my eyes closed. Was there anything like the scent of an apple orchard in spring?

The sound of hooves rustled me from the daze I was slipping into, and I sat forward, gripping with one hand the branch that held me. It was a natural movement, for though I could see through the trees on the other side of the low fence, the angle of the sunlight meant no one on the dappled path could see me. That would change this afternoon, but for now, I could be nosy.

Though there was really no need. Thomas and his men were long gone, escaped deep into Vassian, and the Meirdrean army was now, as far as I was concerned, on my side. Perhaps I only wanted to see if there was any of that girl I used to be left. I was up in a tree, yes, but Laurent should have expected *that* much of me.

The horses drew closer in the dense thicket. It wasn't the principal route to anywhere, but it *was* one of the few stands of dense trees here in the moors, and that was why Thomas's resistance group had always used it to bypass the village. Merchants certainly didn't come through here—the trail was too narrow for all but the narrowest of carts, especially when they could take the main road through the grasslands. We occasionally saw local farmers, yes, but this time of year, few had reason to be on the edge of the Caballero's farm.

I bit my lip. Yes, I'd walked by a few newly planted saplings on my way here, and Elternow was still poor enough that thievery was an ever-present problem. Even of young trees.

The tree cooperated with its silence as I climbed one branch higher, anxious at the idea of a bandit seeing me up here. For the first time, I regretted not telling Captain Erstad where I'd disappeared to. I tucked my knees under myself and leaned back, easing myself against the branch and in line with a hole in the leaves and blossoms. From this position, I could see the bare dirt of the trail, though the horses were far enough away that I still couldn't see them—or their riders.

A whistle cut through the orchard, and the hooves stopped. My palms grew damp, pressed against the branches. Had they seen me? Brown though it was, my dress would be noticeable from a distance, but the limbs had to be breaking up the outline of my figure. The fence that marked the edge of the Caballero's property sat in the middle of a belt of grass, filled with wildflowers, between the end of the orchard and the beginning of the thicket, but was it enough distance to hide me?

One of the horses whinnied, and leather slapped against leather. I sat there, my breath ragged. Someone called the group to a halt, and they dismounted and tossed the reins over their saddles. I glanced toward the Caballero's cottage, but at this distance it was a scarcely noticeable speck in the distance. No help would come from that direction.

Boots thudded in the dirt, louder by the second, and I risked a glance through the apple tree. The man who appeared from between the trees was slight, almost willowy. His shoulder-length hair, bleached by the sun, was loose and disheveled.

I recognized him at once.

Thomas.

CHAPTER FOUR

I HELD MY BREATH AS THOMAS STEPPED INTO the open, his palm flat on the pommel of his sword. He glanced upward, and I went as still as a deer cornered by a hunter, frozen in the complete certainty of my impending death. How had I been so thoughtless as to come here alone? It seemed the dozenth time that very reprimand had flitted into my mind since I'd climbed up here, and I bit my cheek. Berating myself would do no good with him this close. I needed to *think* before he found me, not waste time on pointless admonishments.

But no. As I silently berated myself, Thomas turned back to the thicket and the trail, and then I realized—

He was *remembering*.

He knew this tree, recognized it just as easily as I had. And he—he had cared enough to stop and look at it once more? I hated seeing that humanity in him.

Or was he plotting his revenge?

With a whistle, the horses moved once more, and I sank against my branch, trembling like the very leaves above me. I needed to run back to Mama and Papa's house, needed to alert Captain Erstad about what I'd seen, but my body wouldn't let me move, much less climb down. I sat there for a moment, my breath heavy. By the time the sound of hooves was replaced by the lone wind in the orchard, my heart had returned to normal, and I slid down the tree.

My feet hit the ground, soft underneath me, but before I could walk back toward the cottage, an unyielding hand seized my forearm. My heart thumped widely, whipping away the calm I'd found when I'd climbed down. I opened my mouth to scream, and a hand slammed over my lips.

"They're returning. Back up the tree and do not come down."

Papa's voice was soft in my ear. Soft but firm, with no room for argument. I nodded, then put a hand on the trunk. It seemed to waver in front of me, and I closed my eyes.

"Now!" he whispered, giving me a shove.

I clambered upward as the whinny of a horse filled my ears. They'd approached silently this time, and fool that I was, I hadn't been paying any attention. I glanced down. Papa bustled around the base of a tree farther down the row, yanking out weeds and tossing them into a pile. He looked so comfortable at work that I wondered if he'd been working at the Caballero's for a while now.

"Master Kaleveld!"

Thomas's voice echoed through the orchard, and Papa straightened.

"Hello, Thomas." His greeting was oddly normal. "It's been a long while."

I didn't want to move, certain Thomas would notice me if I did, but I needed a better view. Carefully, I shifted against the branch, sending a shower of petals to the ground. Papa and Thomas were only a few paces apart, and though Thomas's hand was no longer on his sword, he'd lost my trust a long time ago.

"Almost a year, I should think. What're you doing in the Caballero orchard?" He glanced at Papa's hands, the now-nimble fingers no longer red with inflammation. "I'm surprised you can handle manual labor."

Papa grunted and turned away, heaving

an empty apple crate to the other side of the tree. "Found some medicine that worked."

"Ah." Thomas sauntered toward him, his back to me now. "Miracle, that. In Elternow, of all places."

"Traders come through," Papa replied. "Even through Elternow."

"Then you're doing better. I'm happy to hear it."

The flat edge of his sword struck Papa's stomach. I hadn't even seen his hand move. Had I blinked? Was it the sudden tears that had hid his movement? Clinging to the branch, I choked down a scream. Letting go would be so easy. Falling to the ground and punching his face would be delightful—but it didn't look like he was bluffing with that sword.

"You don't have to rob me, Thomas." Papa lifted his hands to his sides. "If you need help—"

"Where is she?"

Papa's forehead creased. "Back at the cottage, of course. The spring onions are ready for harvest."

"Don't play stupid." Thomas took another step forward.

"If you're asking about Riette, she left a long time ago. You've seen her more often than we have, I hear. We get letters, sometimes—not nearly as many as I'd like. That's it."

Thomas's head swiveled behind him, toward the horses and who knew how many other rebels still hidden in the thicket. Did Papa actually think he was fooling him? I didn't know. Perhaps Thomas would believe him, since the soldiers and horses were still back at the house. The only thing I was sure of was that holding my breath was making me dizzy, so I took a few slow, deep ones, praying the breeze hid the sound.

When I looked down again, two other men had joined Thomas. Both too solidly built for anyone in Elternow, both with swords far beyond what I'd ever seen outside of Lochfeld. They hadn't drawn them yet, but when Thomas murmured under his breath and they darted back toward the horses, my stomach grew even tighter. Instructions, certainly, but for what? I twisted toward the thicket, trying to count how many had just ridden off again.

A grunt echoed through my tree. Thomas cleared the fence in one jump and disappeared into the thicket. I couldn't see his horse, but dirt flew into the air as it galloped down the road after its companions. Once it settled on the ground, I decided they were far enough down the road that I could descend, and I scrambled down the trunk, shaking.

"Riette?"

Papa sounded weak, shocked, laying on his side under the apple tree where he'd been pretending to work. For a moment I thought

Thomas had shoved him, or that he'd fallen, but as I knelt to help him sit up, a red stain appeared on his shirt.

My stomach lurched.

"Lay back," I said, ripping open his shirt. The wound didn't look deep, but I couldn't go digging around in it, not after climbing a tree. "I'll get help."

I had no idea how. Mama and the safety of the cottage were all the way on the other side of the farm. Skylark wasn't here. And there was so much blood . . .

"I—I can walk."

He tried to sit, and I gently pushed him back down, then stood.

"No. I'll get a horse."

Without looking back, I darted through the orchard, stumbling over the odd rock and fallen branch. A band of smoke drifted through, lifting the falling petals into the air, and I wrinkled my nose. If the Caballeros were burning something, though I couldn't imagine what they'd be burning on a spring morning, they'd be closer than Mama.

"Master Caballero?" I yelled. "Is that you?"

Fresh earth joined the scent of smoke and apple blossoms. I ducked behind a tree as a horse—no, two horses—appeared at the end of the orchard. If Thomas and his men had circled around to trap us—there would be no way out for Papa or me.

I swallowed, hard. I'd made noise. I'd told them exactly where to find me.

The hooves grew louder in the uneven dirt. I couldn't stay here, pressed against this tree, but I couldn't move forward, either. The smoke grew thicker, not a band now, but a haze that filled the orchard.

And then, too close, the whinny of a horse.

Skylark.

I dashed toward her and grabbed her reins, too surprised to care who might be on the second. But it was Captain Erstad who stared down at me, his own sword drawn.

"Your parents' house is on fire," he said, half out of breath. "And no one could find you."

"Mama?"

"Safe, for now." His horse did an odd side-step. "But the house isn't."

"Thomas Wennink did it. Or his men." I looked down the row of trees and coughed. "And Papa—you have to help him!"

Erstad disappeared toward fresher air without asking questions, and I led Skylark toward him and Papa, unable to move enough to ride her. Papa had somehow managed to lean himself against a tree, though his hands were covered in blood, and I held back as the captain gave him a brief examination.

"How is he?" I asked, gripping Skylark's reins. "Will he—"

"Could be worse." Erstad hefted him up

and onto the back of his own horse. "We'll get him to . . ." He trailed off, likely realizing if there *was* a doctor in Elternow, he certainly wouldn't be visiting Mama and Papa's house any longer.

"There's an inn." I tried to mount Skylark and succeeded that time. Obliging as she was, she didn't react to my less-than-graceful motion. "Small, but they won't be looking for us there—at least for a while. And it's not far if we take the forest path."

Erstad shook his head and pointed back through the orchard where the thick smoke was settling to the ground.

"They might be waiting for us in the woods. We'll take the long way."

I wanted to argue that Papa wouldn't last that long, but Erstad was right. So I clicked my tongue at Skylark, and we set off as the smoke grew thicker around us.

CHAPTER FIVE

THE INN AT ELTERNOW WAS NOTHING LIKE the luxurious inns Juliana and I had stayed at on our way to Iraela not so long ago. Only one fireplace illuminated the roughspun linens on the narrow bed in our room, so after I heated some water, I settled in a corner and watched the midwife work. A doctor, as Erstad had likely guessed, was as common in Elternow as gold coins. But it seemed her services might be enough, for Papa had been conscious enough to order

Mama downstairs, saying her pacing was making everything worse.

I put my head in my hands and closed my eyes. I smelled like a smoldering grass fire—we all smelled the same—but bathing was the last thing on my mind. Even though the wound had turned out to be superficial, a warning slash instead of a fatal stab, infection was always a worry. The scent of balsam from the midwife's poultice overtook the smoke, and I shifted.

"He'll be fine, though in pain for a while." The midwife stood, wiping bloody hands on her white over-apron. "No farm work. And no rebuilding."

Papa opened his mouth, and I hurried to his side before he could argue.

"We'll figure out what to do about the house," I said, my hand hovering over the bandage on his stomach. Shirtless, his injury looked far worse than the midwife claimed. "If nothing else, you can come to Lochfeld."

I hadn't visited the cottage since the fire, but Erstad had seen it with his own eyes. *A smoky pile of wood and thatch,* he'd said. Even the barn was gone, though the soldiers had released the horses before dashing after the arsonist—who'd escaped once they'd returned in an attempt to douse the fire. No one had been injured, not even Papa's prized sow, but the message Thomas's men had left was clear.

We will destroy anything King Laurent has paid for.

"I won't." Papa's eyes steeled. "I won't go there."

"You'll be safer."

"Safe," he scoffed, wincing. "Thomas has done what he wanted in Elternow. He'll head for Lochfeld next."

I knew he was right, but that didn't make leaving any easier. I sank to the bed next to him and grabbed his hand.

"You know I have to return. And I—" A

tear landed on his hand, and I brushed it away. "I've missed you. I need to know you're safe."

"We will be." Papa winced as he shifted. "I swear to you. If that means leaving Elternow, we will find somewhere. Your mother has relatives outside of Harnow who might be willing."

Erstad cleared his throat before I could object to a wagon ride all the way to Harnow. "If that's the case," he said, "we must ride for Lochfeld immediately, Your Grace. Master Kaleveld is correct—once you're gone, Wennink will have no reason to return to Elternow."

"And once we return?" I asked, gripping Papa's hand like I'd never let it go. "Won't he be there?"

"He broke through the castle's defenses once. That will not happen again." Only a hint of disdain dripped from his voice. "We are better prepared this time, with much greater reinforcements. But Wennink and his men were headed south as we pursued them, likely back to Vassian. Even if they turn around, they won't make it to Lochfeld before we do—which is why we must leave at once."

"Can I see Mama first?" There was no way I could leave without saying goodbye, not after she'd lost her home and almost Papa.

"I'm sorry, Your Grace, but we must ride. Your mare is outside and waiting."

I sighed as I nodded and stood. Duty was . . . it was heartbreaking, sometimes. Since I'd married Laurent, duty had seemed dull, sometimes frightening, but I'd never expected it to involve this kind of emotion. Even watching the map had involved dancing, and therefore a tiny of joy.

But this—somehow it was worse than when I'd walked out of their house that winter's night. I'd hope then that I would see them again. Hadn't been certain, though I'd hoped. But now?

It didn't matter. There was only one thing left to do. And so before I could cling to him like a child and refuse to leave, I kissed Papa's cheek and walked out.

The acrid smell of smoke hung about me for the first few hours. After that, I could only smell my own sweat. Erstad had wanted to push the horses at first, to put as much distance between us and Elternow as possible, and by the time we stopped at a pond for rest and water, I could scarcely stand, either.

Knowing I would waste too much time floating aimlessly in the water if I went all the way in, I splashed a bit on my face. On the other side of the pond, the soldiers were filling water bags—probably a more efficient use of our time, but I couldn't help my vanity. As my legs stiffened, I eased myself to the ground and looked up at the sky, crisscrossed with feathery clouds. It was hardly a ladylike position, but the reeds block me from the soldiers' view, and I needed the break.

A piece of hay hit my nose, carried on the breeze from some farm or another, and I twisted backward, trying to find the source. On the other side of a narrow creek, one that could scarcely be called a ditch, lay a fallow field. Odd for spring in an area of the kingdom where empty fields meant empty bellies. Risky, yes, but we did what we had to in Meirdre.

I pushed myself up and meandered toward the open area, crossing a creek on a few large stones. When I'd brushed off Erstad's questions about the haystacks earlier, I hadn't actually let it go—but the fire and Thomas's attack on Papa had distracted me too much to worry about it until now.

There were no stacks in this field, however, and feeling foolish, I turned back toward the pond and prepared myself for another few hours of pretending I was comfortable on Skylark's back. Erstad waved at me from across the pond, and I picked up my damp skirts so I could hurry back.

It was then I noticed the hay. Not piled up, no, but enough was scattered on the ground that I knelt down and examined it. Black streaks ran along the length, confirming the suspicion of mold. I sniffed at it. It didn't smell like smoke, but then again, I could hardly tell if anything did, grimy as I was. Erstad waved at me again, so I grabbed a handful and made my way back.

"Does this look burned to you?" I asked, brandishing the hay in front of him.

"I—" His nose wrinkled. "No, Your Grace. Should it?"

I scanned his face, but there was no deception there—only confusion. But it wasn't as though *every* soldier in Meirdre would be party to such a thing, would it? Maybe Erstad truly didn't know. It didn't exonerate the army. It didn't make Thomas's accusation false.

"Yes." My hands shook, and I shoved the hay closer to his face. Perhaps catching him off guard would force him to confess. "You've been burning hay stores all over the kingdom, haven't you?"

"Your Grace—" Erstad grabbed the straw from my hands. "This is stem rot."

"Stem rot?"

"A fungus, specific to alfalfa and ryegrass. It'll absolutely destroy crops if it becomes established, haystacks especially. We've fought to keep it out of Meirdre for centuries. Thankfully, it's too heavy to be carried on air currents on like regular mold."

"Keep it out?" The spring afternoon chilled. "Where's it from originally?"

His eyes narrowed. "Vassian, of course."

CHAPTER SIX

So, it was Thomas—or, at least someone he knew—who'd seeded the haystacks with stem rot then lied about it, blaming his own crime on the soldiers. Based on his hostile reaction to my question so long ago, I should have known, and yet something had kept me from fully believing my own eyes. Now though . . . I believed. I believed every terrible thing I'd once suspected about him.

Well trained as she was, Skylark tossed her head in displeasure as I stared off into the distant sunset, Laurent's face at the front of my mind. How had he ever forgiven me for mistrusting him so deeply? I'd accused him of the most heinous things, if only to myself, had run off with a man who'd wanted to kill him, and yet—he'd shown me mercy, though I'd thought otherwise at the time. And Lochfeld had become my home.

We had another day of riding in the morning, so I couldn't see the castle up ahead, but it tugged at me from the northeast, enough that I could tell the road would soon curve to the right. I closed my eyes and let Skylark continue on one of her infrequent trots. She knew where she was going, just like I did. And oh, how I wanted to be there again, too.

A rush of wind blew across my face, and my eyes flew open. I hadn't been homesick for Lochfeld since we'd left. I missed Laurent, yes, and it was painful much of the time, but . . . but Lochfeld?

My breath grew short.

It wasn't the same feeling I'd sensed at the castle in Iraela. Not exactly, at least. Still, I was quite sure it was the map—a gnawing hunger, an emptiness that even Laurent's absence couldn't match.

It was calling to me.

I wanted to scream at it, to tell it that I wasn't at Lochfeld, and it just *needed to hold on for another day.* I bit my lip instead, hiding my panic as Erstad let his horse drop back beside me.

"Last chance to stop for the night while the ground is still comfortable," he said, retying dark curls at the base of his neck. "If you're willing."

My eyes unfocused as I looked up the road. I wasn't willing. I wanted nothing more than to continue on and reach the map as soon as possible, but none of the horses were capable of that. And Erstad was correct—soon the ground would grow rocky as we approached the cliffs which protected

Lochfeld, and that would mean no sleep for me and less grazing for the horses.

The pull grew weaker, and I blinked. Was the map telling me it was all right to stop?

"Yes," I replied. "Here seems sufficient."

He nodded and trotted off, giving orders to his men. I eased Skylark off the trail and slumped in my saddle. How was I supposed to sleep tonight? Still, as the carriage appeared behind me and I grudgingly climbed inside, I couldn't deny that my exhaustion was warring with the map's pull. I lay back on the seats, fully clothed, and stared at the ceiling.

Silke had traveled. She *had*. Her journals attested to it, over and over. But she'd never said *how* she managed to explore Meirdre and watch the map at the same time. Was it possible it was so obvious that she never thought to write it down? Or was it that secret?

I yawned and rolled to my side. The

flickers of a fire reflected in the carriage, and the encroaching darkness didn't help my mood. How I wanted to be outside, at the edge of the moors I loved so much. But that would not do for the king's wife, even if—even if she needed the land.

Cautiously, I slid to the other side of the carriage and unlatched the door. A soldier paced somewhere in the distance, and I waited until he wandered off to relieve himself before sliding the door open and creeping out to the back of the carriage.

The pull here was even stronger. Not a surprise, since my feet were sinking into the loose soil that Skylark had no difficulty with. Could that be the key? Father Gerritt had said that I needed contact with the land for the map to speak to me, and out here in the moors, with the moonlight spilling across the carriage, I was closer than ever. Short of having dug through the frozen dirt for rotten potatoes as a child, that was.

Or had Silke simple not cared what happened to Meirdre? Maybe she'd convinced her husband she could read the map while away from Lochfeld, and he'd simply been fool enough to believe her. She hadn't seemed too enamored with her king, and maybe that disinterest extended to Meirdre itself. Maybe there'd been more threats during his reign than she'd written about, and she'd ignored most of them.

I leaned against the carriage, my jaw tight. Perhaps Silke had been wrong. I'd meant it when I'd told Laurent that if staying at Lochfeld forever was what I needed to do, then I would. Yet I'd already broken that vow, was stranded over six hours away from the castle and that vexing map, which was calling for me once more. Yes, it had glowed blue and gold before, showing the next disaster was a few months away, but what if I'd missed something prior to that? I'd assumed seeing the prediction meant things would be safe for a while, but I'd missed something when I was in Iraela, after all. When would *that* disaster happen? Before or after the Vassian invasion?

Silly girl. You have no idea.

The shouts around the campfire grew louder, spurred on, I assumed, by liquor. I wandered away from the carriage as they did, easing my muscles into a painless stroll. The moon bestowed a shimmering path as I drew farther and farther away, until the crackle of the fire and gleeful roars were drowned out by the wind of the moor. Here, at the edge of the grasslands, the land had become rocky, and soon I found myself scrambling over the top of a small rise in the moonlight, the pull of the map too strong to resist. Stars flickered above me, thrown there at the beginning of time, innumerable and eternal. And—and something brighter ahead of me?

A campfire.

I sank to the ground, too conscious that the moon's radiance illuminated everything between here and Lochfeld itself. But that was fine—it also meant I could see the horses down below, grazing while their riders hurried about. Merchants? Tradesmen? I couldn't tell from up here, and their voices were hidden in the soft whispers of the night breeze.

For almost an hour I sat there, waiting for Erstad to realize I was missing, waiting for the travelers down below to go to sleep. Perhaps something told me they wouldn't, even as I shivered in the cooling air. The horses, far from as exhausted as I suspected Skylark was, became increasingly agitated, pawing and circling around, until the figures below saddled them.

I held my breath. Who traveled the moors at night, when bandits roamed and the slightest misstep could be fatal?

Even as I asked myself the question, I knew the answer.

Scrambling back down the hill, I considered my options. Waiting was not among them. Neither was telling Captain Erstad, for a reason I couldn't articulate. Probably because he would doubt me, question me, and by the time he *believed* me, Thomas and his men would be long gone toward Lochfeld. I couldn't let that happen.

I skulked back toward the carriage in the moonlight. Skylark had rested for quite a while now—a few hours, if memory served. She couldn't gallop all night, especially across the rocky terrain, but she could get me closer than we'd be if we slept all night and then rode. That would have to be enough.

Skylark nuzzled my hand as I whispered in her ear. Her ears pricked, attracting the attention of the horse next to her, but I gave him a pat on the haunch, and he quieted down. Skylark had no such anxiety as I slid into her back and circled her around the group, debating how I could disappear without being seen—or pursued. The soldiers would give chase if one of their horses vanished down the road, wouldn't they?

"Your Grace!"

I twisted around at Erstad's voice and brought Skylark's impatient saunter to a stop, the lie coming easily to my tongue. "Captain. There's a pond just up the road. Not more than a five-minute ride. I need—I need some time alone. To bathe. Change into something fresh."

He caught Skylark's reins and frowned at me. "Your Grace, it's late."

"Dark," I replied. "Not late. Not especially. And I can't sleep, filthy like this. All I can smell is smoke in that carriage."

He stared up at me, as if he suspected a trap, then his shoulders relaxed. "If you're not back in half an hour, I'm sending someone for you."

I nodded and forced my most demure smile. Skylark reacted at once to a click of my tongue, eager for an evening walk, and we set off down the road, alone and unpursued. The moon rose as we did, and for what might be the last time in a while, I let myself believe I was home in Elternow, going for an evening stroll, secure in the knowledge that a bed awaited me in the morning.

It wasn't until I was twenty minutes away that I realized how fortunate it was that he hadn't realized I had nothing clean to change into.

CHAPTER SEVEN

I'D DRIFTED OFF TO SLEEP SEVERAL TIMES ON Skylark's back, but she was steady enough—or perhaps used enough to my poor riding—that it hadn't seemed to affect her at all. For when Lochfeld came into view atop the cliffs and I yawned once more, she continued as though nothing untoward had happened the night before.

And perhaps for her, it hadn't. She hadn't seen the men down below, preparing for an evening ride, and we hadn't encountered them on the road, either—which meant they'd stayed far away from any potential traffic. Erstad's men hadn't found us either, likely too consumed with finding the non-existent pond to even begin to close in on me.

Skylar and I pulled off the road and into a stand of trees for two horses and a carriage, but they'd turned out to be brazen merchants, likely headed to Haszen, taking advantage of the moonlight to further their journey and avoid overnighting in the Arsele Forest. We were mostly too enlightened in Meirdre to believe in such things as ghouls, but there was enough of a question that merchants and everyone else avoided it at all costs.

The morning sun grew hot on the right side of my face as Skylark trotted on, and I couldn't help but be grateful that Laurent wouldn't see the freckles that would no doubt appear shortly. In love with him, yes, I was that, but I hadn't forgotten, and probably wouldn't ever, how particular he could be. And the king's wife couldn't be seen with *freckles*.

I laughed out loud at the idea of Laurent's reaction to freckles just as the sound of hooves echoed somewhere in front of me. With a gentle tug of the reins, I backed Skylark into the woods once more and held my breath. We were hardly hidden here, but I was counting on the branch in front of my face and the fact that this interloper, like all the rest, was simply traveling Meirdre like anyone would do.

But as I squinted into the sun, the figure turned familiar.

"Lieutenant Vahl!" I shouted.

He brought his horse to a halt as I trotted out of the woods, shame-faced at having arrived without my entourage and in a dress that probably smelled like I'd set myself on fire. But somehow, he didn't look startled to see me—not a surprise, I supposed, for a man who'd first met me when Laurent had locked me up for treason.

"Your Grace." He glanced around and conspicuously behind me. "What are you—"

"I had to get back," I replied. Now that I was close to Lochfeld and no one could stop me, I could tell him what I'd seen. "I saw—there was a group of men and horses, off the road, preparing the ride through the night. And I knew Captain Erstad would never believe me, or at least not take me seriously enough to do anything about it, so I snuck away and rode through the night to get here." He frowned, and I added, even though he wouldn't understand completely, "I had to warn Lochfeld, someone, anyone!"

"But how do you know they were headed for Lochfeld?" His brow furrowed. "They could have been anyone."

"I—"

Oh, heavens. How had I known? Why had I thought the people I'd seen could have possibly included Thomas? Out in the moors in the moonlight, it had made sense, but now, with the castle towering over us in the morning sun, I was less sure. Not certain at all, if I was being honest with myself. Hadn't I passed benign travelers on the road, after all?

"I don't know." I slumped in my saddle. From here I couldn't even see the soldiers patrolling the top of the castle, and the entire situation seemed a dream. "They seemed —threatening."

"Well . . ." His brows raised, and I felt like an idiot. "Then we shouldn't be standing here on the road, should we?"

I shook my head, and then we were off.

Lochfeld was quiet when we arrived at the stables. My muscles protesting my foolishness more than Vahl ever could, I slid off

Skylark and glanced around. No stable boy arrived to take the horses, but then again, it was still early in the morning, and Vahl was obviously under the impression I wouldn't reprimand him for allowing such an oversight. I'd disappeared to Elternow, had abandoned my position without so much as a second thought, so I couldn't blame him for that. Perhaps he'd run off to visit his own family, so I gave Skylark a perfunctory cool down on my own.

Still irritated at the oversight, I climbed the stairs to my room. Vahl knew enough to alert the soldiers before I could tell the rest of the story, and I was vain enough to refuse to tell it while smelling like smoke and horse.

But Sara was also missing. I yanked off my gown and pulled on another, grumbling over my lack of a bath. My hair? I ran my fingers through it, and then a brush, and then gave up. Laurent wasn't here, anyway. Who was I trying to impress?

Even Laurent's mother seemed to be gone, though she was probably on one of her early morning rides. Elsanne was prone to those ever since she'd arrived, and most of the time I suspected she was trying to see how far she got from Lochfeld before the soldiers found her and begged her to return home. I'd always laughed when they did, for it was obvious they were more afraid of her reaction to being caught than failing to follow Laurent's orders regarding her. Eventually she would outrun them or perhaps even out-sly them, and then she'd be back in Iraela before they could do a thing about it.

And then—and then the king of Iraela would have to decide. Continue coercing Laurent into paying a never-ending dowry, or drop the blackmail and fall back into the distance, enjoying the last years of his life with the wife who now knew she was a pawn—yet somehow loved him anyway.

Not that it any of was my business. Not

anymore, at least. I'd done everything I could.

Laughing over Elsanne's continual insistence that she belonged in Iraela, I made my way to the octagonal war room on knees that wouldn't stop shaking from fatigue. It was the longest ride I'd been on in a while, and had I known I'd be in so much discomfort at the end, I might have made a different decision. But it was done now, and I could deal with Erstad's fury later. Well, soon, for there was no doubt he was closing in on Lochfeld soon.

Clenching my teeth, I pushed open the heavy door. Darkness greeted me, so I lit one of the oil lamps and took a breath. No one was here, preparing for what was to come? It made sense, I supposed. I hadn't seen the soldiers up top when Vahl and I had ridden up the cliff trail, just like I hadn't seen them from the ground below, but they had to be up there somewhere. Actually doing something. Not just planning and hiding inside.

Fool.

The word had scarcely dissipated in my mind when the war room blurred around me, a haze of gold sparkles. I cursed under my breath—of course I hadn't thought to bring any water on my night ride through the moors, and unlike Skylark, I hadn't been able to take a five-second break to slurp water from a puddle. Or was it the map calling to me in some peculiar fashion?

Nonsense. It hadn't acted like this since Juliana had first set the crown on my head.

"There you are." Vahl stuck his head inside, a fuzzy shape surrounded by that same gold effervescence. "Captain Erstad just arrived," he said, gesturing me out. "He's in the throne room waiting on your arrival, and—and he's most displeased with your disappearance last night, Your Grace."

"Oh." Through the pain in my head and

my declining vision, I was a child once more, though I couldn't decide if it was my impending chastisement or my complete and utter discomfort with holding an audience in Laurent's seat of power. "Of course."

Vahl trailed behind me as I made my way down the glittering corridor, pretending I didn't care what sort of tongue-lashing I was in for. I'd made it back to Lochfeld, had warned someone of Thomas's approach, hadn't I? Erstad might think he was in charge, but he would have ignored my warning, just like Vahl had at first. I couldn't have that.

Vahl pulled open the door, and I wet my lips with my tongue, preparing to speak first, before Erstad could make a fool of himself, say something that Laurent would never allow of one of his soldiers.

Or at least, I tried.

Because wasn't Erstad standing there in front of the throne, ready to tear into me for my foolishness last night. In fact, it wasn't a soldier at all.

It was Laurent.

Kneeling.

Kneeling?

And—

And Thomas was beside him, a sword at his throat.

CHAPTER EIGHT

FOR A MOMENT I COULD DO NOTHING BUT stare, praying whatever magic that had overtaken me in the war room was responsible for this new vision as well. For I couldn't be seeing what I was seeing. It was a dream, a nightmare, some trick of the map that showed me the future. But even when I'd worn the crown, even when the crownkeeper gift had been bestowed upon me prematurely, I'd been in control of my senses. Confused, yes, but I hadn't suffered from delusions.

Just like I wasn't suffering from them now.

A cry arose in my throat, and Laurent looked up at the sound. The golden sparkles disappeared in an instant, and my stomach clamped down on itself as I stared at him. His right eye was purple and swollen, his wrists chained in front of him. By the look of the bruises, they'd been that way for a while, which meant—it meant something, but when the shimmering magic had fled, so had my ability to think.

Undaunted by Thomas's sword, I rushed toward Laurent and dropped to the floor in front of him. His harsh inhalations grew steady as my fingers touched his skin, but he didn't move, didn't speak, just watched with weary eyes as my hands ran across his shoulders, his chest, his back. Finding no serious injuries, I lay my forehead against his and wept, my palms against his temples.

"Move away from him, Riette."

I froze at the irritation in Thomas's voice.

"No," I replied, squeezing my eyes shut as the tip of his sword tapped against my collarbone. What else could go wrong if I refused? "I won't."

"Then you will die beside him." The sword tapped again. "A fitting end, perhaps, though I once wished for another."

Bile rose in my throat, and it wasn't from the metal there.

"If you wanted to kill us, you'd have done it already."

"Riette, stop."

Laurent's voice was soft as he reached for me. The chains were too short, so I grabbed his hands and clung to them. They were still smooth, minus a few new blisters from riding, and I ran my fingers over his knuckles, knowing and not caring how much it would infuriate Thomas. But somehow, the order made its way into my heart, and I pressed my lips closed.

"That's all it takes for you to do what you're told? A simple order from a despot?" Thomas laughed. "You really have changed."

I glanced up at him, trying to find the boy he'd once been. The one who had climbed apple trees with me before feeding the apples to the neighbor's horses and skipping home for supper. The one who'd once stood between me and a charging bull. Instead, I found nothing but a hardened expression, the deep lines in the skin of a man who'd traded gentle smiles for frowns and hate.

"So have you, Thomas." I glanced around the throne room. Besides Vahl, the duplicitous bastard, there were no other soldiers around, not that their absence comforted me. If they weren't on Vahl's side, they were no doubt dead. Thomas had enough of his own men positioned around the edges of the room to have seen to that. "And somehow, even after everything, I'm still surprised you could lower yourself to this."

"You always were naïve." The sword slid away from Laurent and me, but Thomas didn't sheath it. "What did you think would happen? That you'd marry a king and live happily at Lochfeld forever? Forsake those you grew up with it? Your family?"

Laurent's breath caught. My tears fell again, and that time, he managed to wipe just one finger across my jaw.

"You did, didn't you?" Thomas chuckled. "Well. Let me tell you how it'll actually end. King Damir wants to see him executed as a common criminal, devoid of any dignity. Just think of it, Riette. Dying far from Meirdre, his power usurped, away from any battle which might have preserved his honor in death. And you—"

I tore my gaze from Laurent's anguished stare and met Thomas's.

"You." He tapped his sword on my shoulder. "I would so dearly love to see your blood spilled besides him, but"—glee sprang into his tone—"I'm told you have a gift that might still be considerably useful."

The throne room spun about me once more, but it was a gray haze that had taken over my vision this time. My own terror flowed through me, not a belated enchantment. If I hadn't already been kneeling, I would have collapsed on the floor from the fear and anger and betrayal that seized me, for it was obvious how Thomas had figured that out. I met Laurent's gaze, and he nodded, just enough.

"They were going to—if they found you —" he began. "I had to tell them. Please— please forgive me—"

"He saved your life, Riette," Thomas interrupted, "by telling me your secret. Even as he was condemning his own."

I leaned my forehead against Laurent's once more and tried to steady my voice. What I was about to say would earn me my death, but I didn't want to live anymore. Not without him.

"So what?" I gripped his hands tighter as I spoke. "I don't see what that has to do with you, what you think my power will gain you. It protects Meirdre and her sovereign, no other kingdom, no other person."

"It certainly didn't do a satisfactory job this time." Thomas's lip curled in a sardonic smile. "But regardless, and fortunately for you, King Damir disagrees with your assessment of your inadequacy. He finds your gift . . . rather fascinating."

I swayed as he spoke, certain I would crumple to that luxurious stone floor. It was Laurent who clutched at my hands now, whispering something consolatory in my ear, though the words no longer had any meaning. Not so long ago, I'd knelt in this exact spot, that night Laurent had sentenced me to death—and as horrified as I'd been, being sentenced to life was worse. There had been a pang of regret in Laurent's expression then, even as he'd pronounced the words that would end my very being.

But Thomas displayed no such remorse.

"It only works here." I could scarcely draw a breath. "Only at Lochfeld. If you take us to Vassian, the gift won't follow."

"Is that so?" Thomas snapped his fingers, and Vahl yanked me to my feet. "Then I suppose we'll find out, won't we? Hope you enjoy the voyage."

CHAPTER NINE

I HAD NEVER HAD THE MISFORTUNE OF traveling on a ship before. Laurent, I was certain, had. Nonetheless, almost immediately after they shoved us in a dark hold, he'd become ill, and I'd spent the next few weeks tending to him. No matter how much I tried to cajole Thomas's men for the slightest comfort, they'd refused to anything more than give me a few buckets to relieve ourselves in and a basket of salty, dried fish. That was reassuring, in an odd way, for it meant we wouldn't be aboard this creaking hulk for long.

Not that I truly had to wonder. Too weak to give details, Laurent had been vague about how he'd ended up back at Lochfeld after heading to the Vassian border, but I knew the army of Meirdre would have spread throughout the kingdom looking for him by now. Taking us to Vassian by sea, sailing down the coast and past our borders, avoiding our army, was the safest route for Thomas.

I soaked a piece of cloth in what little condensation I could find on the wood above my head, then lay it over Laurent's head. He'd curled up in the corner of the hold a few hours ago, and although he'd refused the fish, his stomach seemed to have settled. Perhaps the waves had subsided as well, but I wouldn't let myself think of what that meant.

"I will never forgive myself," he whispered, as I leaned against him, "for not being the one to take care of you."

I forced a laugh. "I'm happy to be healthy enough to be able to do it. We needed a bit of luck."

"I wouldn't call this luck, Riette, dear."

"I suppose not." His forehead was warm under my palm, even though the rag was cool. "But I'm still glad I'm with you."

Laurent pressed his lips together. "I am not."

"I know. But—" He didn't ask for clarification of my lingering silence, and my eyes grew wet. "But I couldn't have stood it if you'd disappeared and I had no idea of what happened to you."

"I don't think you want to find out what happens to me now."

I didn't. I couldn't even bear to think of it. Shifting on the hard wood behind my back, I squeezed his hand.

"The map never warned me of this," I

said. Was the magic gone? Had it abandoned me? Or was it true, like I'd said to Thomas, that it didn't work outside the borders of Meirdre? "Perhaps—"

Metal clanging above interrupted my thoughts. A shaft of light fell across my grimy dress as the trapdoor slid to the side and a man dropped a rope ladder to the floor.

"He wants to talk to you." He pointed down at me, his Vassian accent strident and authoritative. "Up."

Laurent made a noise of disapproval, but I didn't look at him as I stood. If I did, I would cling to him, and while I wanted to do that, I wanted to know what *he*—likely Thomas—wanted to talk to me about. So raising my chin, I lifted my skirts, and climbed the ladder as gracefully as I could.

The warm breeze caught my hair almost immediately, carrying with it the briny scent of the ocean. Over the edge of the deck, the faint darkness on the horizon signaled land —but then again, we wouldn't have had to sail very far east to sail down the coast unnoticed. But the recent serenity of the waves and Thomas's summons didn't lie, and I was certain we were almost to Vassian, if not within its waters already. If only my knowledge of maps went deeper than the one on the floor of the ballroom at Lochfeld.

The man motioned me through a doorway in the center of the ship, a shadowy and cool compartment, lined with windows. The wool carpet was soft under my feet, the exact color of the glassy ocean outside, and a rich silk printed with sea dragons lined the slender walls which remained in between the glass. It was a bit of royalty, right here in the middle of the sea.

But instead of the ship's captain, who doubtless occupied this space in normal times, Thomas was sprawled in a velvet chair against the far window, a grin on his face and his boots propped up on the desk in front of him. He hadn't bothered to move the charts underneath his feet, and I couldn't help but wonder if the captain knew. Thomas's shoulder-length hair was cleaner than I suspected it had been for some time, and I hated him even more for being clean when I was not.

"You don't look well, Riette," he greeted me. "It's amazing what such an extensive lack of sunlight does to a person."

"You deserved it," I spat at him. "And more. But I fought for your life anyway, and this—this is how you repaid me for that mercy? Repaid him?"

"Mercy?" His tone was sharp as he sat forward. "What would you know of mercy? What would you know of a dungeon under that castle? Of scarcely being able to sit, so restricting was your confinement? Of being so thirsty you could hardly speak?"

I wanted to retort that Thomas being

hardly able to speak was likely a boon to everyone in Lochfeld's dungeon, prisoner and jailer alike, but I held my tongue.

"No," he went on, as I stood there, my jaw tight. "I don't suppose you know anything about mercy. And so I shall show him none."

My heart disappeared somewhere I couldn't feel it any longer. I knew beyond a doubt that Laurent's future was short, and likely painful, but accepting it? I couldn't accept it. Yes, his decision to not release Thomas was cruel, and from time to time I still had nightmares about the moans I'd heard in that cell when I'd left the dungeon myself, but . . . there was mercy there, too. For Thomas *was* a traitor. And he'd deserved death, just as I had, I suppose. Had worked to overthrow Meirdre, and Laurent had done what he'd done to save it. Even to save me and Thomas and ourselves, for weren't we part of Meirdre?

"I won't plead with you," I replied. I

wanted to. Oh, heavens, I wanted to. Pleading my own life, no, that I would never do. But pleading for Laurent's? Yes, I would have done that if I'd thought it would make one bit of difference. "If that's what you're looking for, then you've called me here for nothing at all."

"I wouldn't go that far." He reclined once more, lifting his boots back onto the desk. "I want to talk to you."

"About what?" I ground out, clenching my hands behind my back. It occurred to me that it was the same way I used to stand before Laurent. I'd always thought it was fear, but now I realized it was anger.

Thomas folded his hands behind his head and regarded me.

"About your future."

My eyes burned, but I blinked away the tears. It occurred to me, for the first time since I'd entered, that I was still standing just inside the cabin like a fool, frozen. Like a deer who'd caught the scent of a hunter in the small stands of trees around Elternow.

"What about it?" I asked, stepping forward. "I was led to believe I didn't have one."

He cocked his head. "That depends, of course."

Of course.

If Lochfeld's magic worked for the king of Vassian, I would be a slave, doomed to spend a lonely existence in exile, away from the castle I'd grown to appreciate, far from my parents, unable to mourn the husband I never thought I'd love. Lonely, confined, captive to a foreign king who hated me and everything I cared about.

Or would it be so lonely?

My blood ran cold, even though the ocean breeze through the open door was warm, and sun spilled through the countless windows.

"Depends on what?" I asked.

Thomas's lips curved, revealing teeth

stained with tobacco. I'd smelled it when I stepped inside, and it hadn't bothered me then, but that was back when I'd imagined a kindly sea captain smoking a pipe and staring at maps.

"You shouldn't worry about what's coming," he said, examining his nails. "Yes, it's true that if you turn out to be of use to Vassian, you will have to remain there for the rest of your life—but that life needn't be excruciating. I would be willing to shield you, shall we say, from some of the worst parts of your captivity. It's the least I can do as an old friend, someone who you once cared for. Though, naturally," he went on, "that depends on your ability to help His Majesty. If, as you claim, the magic is limited to Lochfeld, there's nothing even I can argue that would save you."

"I don't want anything from you."

His sharp gaze focused on me. "That's rather short-sighted, don't you think?"

I shook my head and glanced out the window. A gull floated there, hovering on the breeze. Past it, the horizon darkened, darkening my soul at the same time. Without saying goodbye to Thomas—without even acknowledging him—I turned and strode out of the captain's cabin. No one stopped me, not even the man who'd ordered me up from the hold, so I wandered to the side and looked over the edge.

The sea was shallow here, clear and vibrant with fish and colored rock. I could see all the way to the sandy bottom, covered in the shells, the remains of sea creatures that had been smashed upon the waves. They hadn't wanted to die either, but nature was cruel. Human nature—or at least the men who had control of mine now—was even crueler.

And shallow or not, my feet would never reach the bottom. Jumping would be so easy. They might come after me, but I could fight them off—or at least use their own weight in my favor. I wouldn't have to see Laurent murdered, I wouldn't have to stand there and be tested by a man I feared and despised, I wouldn't have to toil for him for the rest of my life, betraying and annihilating my kingdom.

A shadow fell across my hands as they gripped the side, feeling the splinters where the wood had been abraded by whatever work sailors did on a ship. I shoved my palm against one of the larger splinters, flinching as it plunged into my skin. Rash, yes, but just like when I'd almost destroyed my fingers trying to undo the shackles in Lochfeld's dungeons, it wouldn't matter soon. I wouldn't live long enough to die of infection.

"Riette." Thomas spoke too close, too plaintively, though he didn't touch me. "Come back inside."

I shook my head and braced myself.

Please forgive me.

I lifted my right foot, but before I could place it against the railing, the calm sea of five minutes ago disappeared in an unnatural rush of whitecaps, sending the ship rolling sideways and propelling me backward a step. My face damp with sea spray, I ground my feet into the deck and sprang for the railing once more, but the ship rolled to the left, and I tumbled sideways, straight into Thomas's arms. He grabbed my wrist as I tried to yank it away, then jerked my arm behind me.

"Dammit, Riette, don't be stupid!"

I shrieked at him to let me go, but he clung to me as I kicked at him, fighting to reach the side once more. His grip grew tighter as he dragged me to the center of the deck, and for a moment I heard actual fear in his voice. In confusion, I stopped. The ship swayed backward, and smooth glass replaced the waves that had been there just a moment before. I let myself sag in his grip, heavy reality overcoming my desperate desire to flee.

What would jumping accomplish? Laurent's fate was certain, yes, but—but I couldn't leave him to it alone. I couldn't betray him like that. I wouldn't allow him to die alone, especially if that was what Thomas and the king of Vassian wanted. I shoved my elbow into Thomas's side, and that time he stepped away, but not before giving me a wary look.

"Take me back to him," I ordered. "Now."

"Riette, look, it doesn't have to be this way. You can—"

"I will not abandon him." My voice shook as I interrupted him, turning toward the hatch that led to the hold. "Not now."

Not ever.

CHAPTER TEN

THERE WAS NO ROOF ON THE CART THAT DREW us through the streets of the seaport village where we'd landed to the minor castle on the cliffs above. Soldiers in brilliant red uniforms, gaudier than anything anyone in Meirdre would ever consider wearing, rode alongside us. They were ostensibly to protect us from the residents who'd gathered to see the condemned king of Meirdre hauled to his death, but protecting our lives was all they appeared to be doing. They certainly weren't doing much to deflect the rotten vegetables and small stones being hurled at the cart.

Laurent drew me against him as another rock landed by my feet. It bounced off the shoes I'd been given, but I was lucky—Laurent's exposed skin showed bruises. Some of his former strength seemed to have appeared since we'd disembarked at the wharf, though he still looked pale and drawn. The shackles around his wrists ground against the back of my neck as he held me, but I didn't complain. King or prisoner—or both, I supposed—I felt safe with his arms around me, even in such a place.

"I love you," he murmured against my hair. "I am furious you're here, but heavens, sometimes it seems a miracle at the same time." He sucked in a breath, then pushed my face against his chest, a hand on the back of my head.

"What happened?" I mumbled. "Let me see!"

"Just a rock." I strained to free myself to check on his injuries, but he held me tight and ran his fingers through my hair. "There will be more. Don't trouble yourself with a bit of blood, my dear."

"They can't do this." I'd been saying it since we left the wharf, but I'd say it once more, like it could change something. "They can't."

"Damir has been wanting Meirdre for years. At least a decade." He took another breath, but that time I didn't fight to see what had happened. "We stand in the way of his movement toward Nantoise and beyond, always have. But I will not surrender our access to the sea by retreating to the west like my father always spoke of doing."

"He did?" I chewed on my lip. West of the Tourmel Mountains, Meirdre sprawled for days, but Laurent was right—access to the ocean was too important to concede. The castle above Windersay, where the cart was now dragging us, was enough proof of that—Vassian's own watch of the coast. And how could I forget that Elternow sat right where Damir would march on his way north? Lochfeld, as well. Had my parents made it somewhere safe? Would Thomas find them if Vassian took our kingdom? They would have to become almost invisible to hide from his retribution.

"Damir spoke of a treaty, some years ago. Give up the kingdom east of the mountains, and all threats of war cease." Laurent sighed and loosened his grip so I could see the fortress ahead of us.

It menaced above us on the hill, ever so close now, stone and cannons and a flag I'd never seen before. It took my breath away, and I had to remind myself that this wasn't even the principal castle of King Damir—just an old garrison turned royal abode a century ago, kept for its view of the sea. From there, his soldiers could see—and repel—any invasion from the east.

"But I refused to order my people to emigrate," he continued, "to leave their homes to be burned and eventually taken by the enemy. I assumed if I put up a strong enough fight at the beginning, the threats would cease."

I didn't bother mentioning his deal with Iraela that had plunged Lochfeld into near-poverty and nearly destroyed our fledgling marriage. Or that it was, technically, still in place. Maybe it had seemed a lesser evil to a king threatened with invasion on all sides.

"Is there still a chance? For a treaty, I mean?"

He was silent for a while, and I hated it, because it made the shouts of the villagers impossible to ignore.

"No," he replied at long last. "The time for talking, for agreements, for peace, is past. I have infuriated him with my refusals, clearly"—this with an intentional rattle of the shackles—"and he will not stop until he sees all of Meirdre burned to the ground, her people destroyed. I'm only the first of many, Riette."

"But what about me?" I whispered. It was childish and selfish, but he had to make everything better. He *had* to. I still trusted him that much, even after everything. Because if he loved me, if he wanted forgiveness, he would make everything right, wouldn't he? "What's going to happen to me? Why did you tell him about the map?"

"You would have been right there beside me, otherwise, a sword at the back of your head." Laurent shifted on the hard bench as the shouts grew quieter once more. "I had no choice. If I couldn't save Meirdre, at least I could save you. And then perhaps one day, you can fight to get her back."

"That's ridiculous." I choked out a bitter

laugh. "You don't know what you're talking about."

"You dare call your sovereign's wish ridiculous?" If my statement had been harsh, his reply was castigatory. For the briefest moment I wasn't in the cart, clinging to him like a child, but in front of him in the throne room at Lochfeld, a peasant girl, a subject, his to order about as he pleased. "You will do what I ask of you, you will do it immediately, and you will not question it."

I pulled away and stared at him, heedless of the moldy apple that had fallen to the bench beside me. Protecting me had come at a cost. Blood oozed from a cut on his jawline, and a bruise was forming on his left cheekbone, but that wasn't what kept me frozen with fear.

It was his eyes.

They weren't dull with inevitability, like I suspected mine were. They were full of . . . well, not hate, not exactly. Laurent had never let such banal things as hate color his view of the world. Fury, yes. Maybe. I couldn't deny that I felt the same. But there was something more than that, even. Hard—they were simply hard. Not with fear, but with arrogance.

My heart sank. This wasn't the man I'd fallen in love with. It was the king I'd feared when I first met him, who'd laughed at me when I'd stood up to him and ordered me whipped when I'd betrayed his trust. And I knew then—this was the only way he could die with his dignity intact. And if he needed to pretend, then I would as well. I owed him that much, and he deserved that much.

I lifted my head as the horses slowed to pass under the portcullis. The bailey was filled more soldiers than I could count, and when the cart stopped, I slid away from him and gripped the edges of the bench.

"What else would you order of me, sire?" I asked.

It felt like I was questioning a stranger. Perhaps I was. Maybe I'd never really known him, and the brief emotion I'd felt toward him had been nothing more than my imagination. Wishful thinking. The pretending of a girl who knew the world was against her and tried anyway.

Laurent stared off into the distance, over the battlements and into the woods that surrounded them. Fog hung in the trees, shrouding the rear of the structure in mist. I imagined it was a good defense—on cooler days, the castle probably disappeared into the fog, invisible to invading ships until it was too late. The cannons above us certainly saw to that.

"Whatever they ask of you," he replied finally.

Even as I climbed the low, stone stairs in the keep, soldiers in front of and behind me, I wondered why they'd brought us here, instead of to Damir's main castle, far to the south in the capital of Vassian. Was this simply a stop, a place convenient to the sea where they could regroup, pack supplies, and continue the journey later? Or was it to end here? The shadows cast by the oil lamps seemed to imply a dark future, one I still couldn't accept.

Laurent was no longer with me. The soldiers had dragged him away as soon as I'd scrambled from the cart, and he hadn't fought them. I had tried to fight my escorts, but no sooner had I jerked my elbow away from the nearest soldier than Laurent's words echoed in my mind.

Whatever they ask of you.

I still wasn't entirely sure I agreed with this command, but asking me to scale a few flights of stairs seemed harmless compared to everything else that had and would happen, so I let myself be ushered into the tower, and now, toward the top. The overwhelming constraint of the structure and lack of windows made my physical situation even clearer than before. Seawater soaked the bottom of my gown, and the rest hadn't fared much better. I couldn't decide whether it was the slime I'd acquired in the ship's hold or the rotten fruit which stuck to the fabric, but I smelled worse than I ever had as a farmer's daughter. Even cow manure had a certain sweetness to it that I now lacked.

I was to face Damir like this, certainly. Maybe that was a blessing in disguise, for what man would believe a woman who looked anything like I did would be capable of any kind of magic? But then, if I lied . . . I forfeited my life.

My breath grew short as my guards knocked on the door on a small landing. They swung it open without invitation, and sunlight streamed across my face. In the dark of the stairwell, I'd already forgotten such a thing as the sun existed, and for a moment I could only blink in the brightness, a headache sparking through my brain. It was a window across the tower room that was responsible for the sudden illumination, and I focused on the sea in the distance.

Freedom.

"You didn't have a pleasant voyage."

The voice, low and accented, shrouded in the shadows beyond a stone column, caught me by surprise. He added a few words, a little louder, in his native language, and the soldiers disappeared.

"I imagine sailing could be undertaken in a more pleasant manner, yes," I replied. I moved to smooth my skirts as the door thudded shut, then stopped. What did it matter? He could already see how dreadful I looked.

"Indeed."

Damir moved into the light then, and I caught my first real glimpse of him. He was certainly older than Laurent, with cropped gray hair above a leathery face. I hated him immediately, more for his age than anything else. How dare he deny Laurent the time that he had enjoyed for so long?

"But such things are unfortunately necessary sometimes," he went on. "Especially when the future of Vassian is at stake."

"I have no real worry for the future of Vassian," I retorted.

"No, you wouldn't." He chuckled. "Nonetheless, I do, and you appear to be the answer to some of my prayers."

Whatever they ask of you.

"And I'm here for you to test me." I wandered toward the stone bench under the window and sat, inhaling the sea breeze. It was a risk to do something so casual in front of a king, but he wasn't *my* king, and I needed to catch my breath. How much longer would I be allowed something as mundane as fresh air? "To see if the rumors are true."

"I don't need to test you. You are a crownkeeper." He held up a hand as I opened my lips, questioning. "Oh, yes, even in Vassian, we've heard of the legends. But some of us believe more than most. Have seen things, even, things that make testing you irrelevant. I know you have a gift."

"How?" My mouth was dry. I'd hoped he would have dismissed me as a charlatan.

"Legends and myths all have some basis in reality—even such things as dragons. And your husband was insistent enough that you could be of use to me. It's not something you could feign for very long, if at all, so I have to believe his claim is true."

"I told Thomas. The magic only works at Lochfeld."

"So he said. But I don't believe that's the truth."

The breeze caught my hair, and even though the spring morning was cool, I was suddenly hot. The sudden waves that had appeared when I'd tried to jump over the side of the ship—had that been the magic? I should have been relieved at the idea of the map protecting me, even from myself, but instead, I felt trapped. More trapped than I'd ever felt at Lochfeld, wondering if I'd ever be able to leave again.

Damir fell to the bench across from me, and though I could feel his stare, I could only focus on my feet and the smell of salt that filled the tower room. Maybe that was the answer to Silke's freedom, so long ago. Perhaps it so was obvious, like I'd once wondered, that she hadn't bothered writing about it. Because if the magic worked at sea, surely it could reach me away from the ballroom. The Creator wasn't limited to Lochfeld, after all.

They can feel when Meirdre is in danger, can

warn of wildfires, border raids, epidemics. And the map speaks to them, shows them where misfortune is happening.

My heart skipped a beat.

Father Gerritt. He'd given me the answer back then, when he'd first told me about crownkeepers, and he hadn't even realized it.

Oh, heavens.

No, that wasn't right. This was Father Gerritt I was talking about. His wording was no mistake—it never was with him. Of course he'd realized it. He had *definitely* known exactly what he had said to me.

They can feel when Meirdre is in danger . . .

Could it be—could it be that it wasn't the map calling to me at all? Could the intense pull I'd experienced have been the magic itself, not calling me back to Lochfeld, necessarily, but simply warning me? The map helped, yes, there was no doubt about that, but I was starting to wonder if it was only one tool in a crownkeeper's armory. Perhaps a more experienced crownkeeper would have a better grip on things, could determine what the *feelings*, as Father Gerritt had called them, meant.

"It is the truth," I gasped, too conscious of Damir's attention on what must be my terrified expression. "The map—it's the only way my gift works."

The sensation of disappointment that flowed over me was immediate. Not from the king, for he merely raised a suspicious eyebrow, but from somewhere else, out past the Galvan Ocean that stretched further than I could imagine, west of Iraela and its palace were Elsanne was doubtless now cavorting with her scheming husband, north of Lochfeld and its map that had introduced me to such power.

I clutched at my chest, not caring what Damir thought. If he thought I was terrified, so be it—for I was that too, in all honestly. But there was also hope, for if I didn't need the map, I could protect Meirdre even as cut off from Lochfeld as I was. But that also meant Damir had a greater chance of using my gift for the glory of Vassian, and I would not allow that. No matter what Laurent had ordered of me.

"If that's so—" He stood and called for the soldiers in that odd language of Vassian. "Then we shall proceed without delay. I do wish things had gone differently, Your Majesty."

I sank against the stone as he disappeared, too devastated to correct him. And in my heart, I knew I could never agree to what Laurent had ordered me to do.

CHAPTER ELEVEN

Regardless of what Damir had said, I knew he hadn't believed my claim. Why would he, when Thomas and Laurent had both suggested the opposite? I struggled with his calm acceptance for hours as the sun circled the tower, leaving my stone bench shrouded in shadows that hadn't been there when the soldiers had locked the door behind the departing king.

The earlier warmth had departed too, and I shivered in my still-damp gown as the breeze through the window cooled. By the time Thomas entered, a hunk of bread in one hand and a flask of water in another, I would have done anything for a blanket and dry shoes. Instead, he took a white dress from a soldier outside and handed that to me as well.

"You expect me to wear this?" I asked.

He closed the door, leaned against it, and nodded toward the dress with his chin. "King Damir wishes you to be suitably attired for the execution."

I dropped the gown to the floor and stared at the shadows swimming in the folds of the silk. White, naturally, and the reason for Damir's choice of the celebratory color was apparent. I was forbidden from mourning. Become a maiden again, as if Laurent had never existed in the first place. And Thomas himself, always one to appreciate the dramatic, was reminding me of what Laurent himself had forced me to wear in the dungeon at Lochfeld.

"I would rather wear what I have on, thank you."

"That is not your choice." In the shadows, his eyes flashed. "You are allowed no preferences anymore—or were your circumstances not clear enough?"

"Thomas." Stepping over the fabric, I held out my hands. "I don't want any food. Or the dress. Or any of this. Please. You can still fix this. If you ever cared one bit for me—please help me. Help us."

He scoffed, and the sound was a dagger through my heart.

"Put it on."

Without releasing his gaze, I picked it up and crept behind a column to change in almost-dark privacy. That was something, and so was the cleanliness of my new garment, even if my stays were filthy. How long had it been since I'd picked them out in my room at Lochfeld? Time had so little meaning anymore.

Thomas gave me—or perhaps the gown— an approving nod when I ventured from behind the stone once more, having disposed of the wet shoes as well. Without a word, he opened the door and motioned me out onto the landing, where six soldiers waited. I stumbled on the threshold, and when I looked up, all seven of them were staring at me with no expression whatsoever.

Any warmth I might have felt upon discarding my wet clothes vanished as I crept down the stairs, surrounded by this group who hated me more than I could comprehend. It wasn't the chill of the evening though, just a desperate, ill feeling. Part of me knew what was waiting for me at the bottom, but part of me refused to imagine the horrors. That refusal, protective as it was, didn't last long enough. Shoved out of the tower and into the bailey, I stumbled in the dirt.

When I looked up, I was thankful I'd declined the bread—and even the water—for Laurent stood in the same wagon that had brought us here, shirtless and calm, his hair blowing in the breeze and hands tied behind his back.

And a rope around his neck.

Like he had ordered of Thomas.

The courtyard spun around me, a blur of oil lamps and darkness and stars. My scream must have surprised Thomas as much as it surprised me, for he didn't flinch until my nails had drawn a long line of blood down his cheek. He grabbed my wrist as I tried once more, but the pain was merely a flash compared to the agony in my soul.

"You bastard." I doubted he could understand my slurred words. "You couldn't just let him die. You had to make a point!"

"I told you at Lochfeld," he said, yanking me against him. "So this should come as no surprise. He will die as a criminal. If it so happens that I can arrange his death as he would have had mine, so much the better. The manner of his death was one of the few favors I asked of King Damir for my service."

"The money wasn't enough?" Dizzy, I sucked in a breath. Behind me, a horse whinnied, and I thought of Skylark, of running through the meadow north of Lochfeld with Laurent by my side. We had been so happy, and I hadn't even realized it. I hadn't appreciated everything he'd given me—not the money, not the luxury, but the gift of his love.

"The money is never enough, Riette. It wasn't for me, and it wasn't for Vahl— though unlike him, I won't be taking my payment and heading for the islands quite yet." Thomas spun me around to face Laurent once more as the gravity of Vahl's betrayal sank in. What a fool I had been to trust someone I'd never really trusted. "You'll walk behind the cart," he whispered in my ear. "Next to King Damir. You will not cry, you will not speak, you will not stall."

Whatever they ask of you.

In a heartbeat, Laurent's order went from foolish to comforting. I tried to wrap my grieving heart around the change, but the horses drawing the carriage began to move, and Thomas shoved me forward. Damir, naturally, did not walk next to me, but rode a stallion, so tall I could scarcely glimpse his ears as I lowered my head and focused on the stones under my bare feet. It was that or watch Laurent, and I couldn't bring myself to watch him be drawn down the hill.

There were no villagers present tonight, no angry Vassian subjects throwing apple cores and stones. I puzzled over their absence as the walk wore on. Surely Damir wouldn't have ordered them away now. But as we proceeded into Windersay proper and through the still-empty streets, I realized where they had gone.

They were waiting in the square, anxious to witness an execution.

I had prayed in the tower that this wasn't the end, and even as I followed Laurent down the road toward the sea, I still hoped. This was the last piece of Damir's puzzle, though—Laurent wouldn't be executed in the capital. No, that kind of infamy alone would bestow too much honor upon him. He would die in this no-name seaport, and few would remember the story once the generation that had witnessed it had passed away. One last humiliation of the king who'd refused to surrender his kingdom.

Thomas jerked me to a stop as I tried to blink back tears, tried to ignore the roar of the crowd. I failed, but my sobbing didn't seem to matter to Damir as his soldiers forced Laurent up the scaffolding ladder. I would have stumbled my way up, but my husband ascended as gracefully as though he was standing from the throne at Lochfeld, then straightened under the gallows. I stared at his composure, and in return his gaze focused on mine for the first time tonight. For a moment I thought his lip curled upward, but before I could question my own crazed imagination, his expression turned blank once more.

Why are you crying, Crownkeeper?

My stomach fluttered. I didn't hear the words, not exactly, but I felt them, somewhere deep, somewhere no one in Vassian could touch. My gaze wavered between the executioner and his assistants, between the rope hanging over the gallows and the whip hanging from his hand, between Laurent's calm visage and the villagers screaming for his blood.

All this, and I hadn't sensed a single threat to the Meirdrean throne.

It made little sense. If Father Gerritt was correct, I should have felt *something*, especially this close to the end of his line and my kingdom. Even if he was mistaken, I should have felt the map calling me, begging me to return to Lochfeld and avail myself of its magic.

But I didn't.

I felt nothing but rage.

Rage tinged with hope.

The executioner raised the whip. A crack echoed through the square, followed by cheers, applause, and shouts of *harder*. Laurent grunted, and I flinched, confusion overcoming my fury and grief. His feet were stable on the platform now, but that would soon change. Even Laurent, strong as he was, couldn't hold out like this for long. There was no rescue coming, no one to save him.

No one except—

A shimmer fell across the scaffolding, almost blinding me. The yearning I'd felt in Iraela took shape once more, tugging my feet forward with unimaginable power. I ground my toes against the stones, earning a quiet and unnatural laugh upon the breeze before the pull resumed. Only this time, instead of calling me toward Lochfeld, it summoned me toward the steps.

No one except me.

A ROAR FILLED MY EARS AS I REACHED THE TOP step, like the thunder that swept over Elternow during the summer storms. But the night was clear, and the stars that watched from high above precluded any rain. Overcome by the sensation of not controlling my body, I didn't turn in the direction of the sound, though the executioner's head swiveled toward the bay. I was close enough to see his throat move as he swallowed, then he backed away from Laurent and waved at Damir. But his attention didn't fall on me.

No, it was somewhere much farther away. Farther even than Damir and the soldiers surrounding him.

The gleeful shouts of the crowd died away, fading to an anxious buzz as I stopped and faced Laurent. Several of the villagers at the back of the group spun around and took off running up the street in the tower's direction, shouting for the rest to follow. I couldn't understand their words through the sound coming from the ocean and the dizziness inside my own brain. Seemingly oblivious to my presence, the executioner dropped the whip and met Damir's eyes. The king nodded, though his glance continually shifted up the cliffs, and the executioner jumped to the cobblestones below, only to dash off into the dark streets.

Laurent blinked at me as he wavered on his feet, silently pleading with me, but some unfamiliar power kept me frozen, just paces away from him. The roar of not-thunder grew louder, joined by hoofbeats, as a flood of horses galloped through the streets, heading for the cliffs. Some drew carts, some carriages, and some only carried frightened villagers, clinging for their lives. I had the vague, indistinct impression that I should follow—or at least grab Laurent and follow—but my feet held as fast to the wood beneath them as though they'd been nailed.

Damir circled the gallows on his horse, his eyes wide with horror—though somehow, there was no shock in his expression. Like he'd known I'd lied, just as he'd accused me of. It was then that I realized *I'd* done something, that whatever the sound was, whatever had caused so much fear throughout the streets of Windersay—

I'd done it.

Damir galloped away as the shimmering light fell away from the scaffolding, the rest of the soldiers behind and around him. The smoke of a hundred torches disappearing along with them filled the square, but I couldn't even turn to watch him flee up the hill. A silence overtook the square as they vanished into the streets, heavy and powerful, broken only by faraway shouts and the distant whinnies of frightened, overloaded horses.

"Riette."

I swayed on top of the scaffolding as Laurent's whisper freed me from my immobilization. The noose still hung heavy around his neck, and I darted toward him, lifting him up the best I could. My fingers pried at the rope securing his hands, but outside of stabbing myself with a thousand splinters, I made little progress in freeing him. A knife, it was a knife I needed, but whatever had frightened everyone off, it hadn't seen fit to leave me with a weapon.

"I can't free you," I sobbed at him. "Not without a knife."

He leaned heavily on me, though not

enough to put any pressure on the noose. I knew I had to leave him, to run into one of the nearest inns or houses and find something I could use, but I couldn't leave him.

"You don't need to." He pointed toward the wharf—at least, as well as one could point with their shoulder. "Look."

Water.

It flowed through the empty streets, rushed past the scaffolding, under our feet. I had heard of such things—huge, violent waves that had devastated our coastal cities in Meirdre long ago, but *this* wave hadn't destroyed anything. It simply surged forward, clear and placid, leaving standing buildings in its wake. A terrified horse that hadn't been seized for the villagers' retreat stood frozen just outside of the plaza, not floundering to its death, but watching the water flow harmlessly about it.

I squinted over the tops of the village, toward the bay. The ships in the harbor must have been destroyed, smashed against the wharf, but masts and sails were visible in the moonlight, floating back and forth as on a windless summer day.

"What is this?" I whispered.

Before he could answer, the water receded, as pure as when it had come. No debris marred the retreating swell, no buildings had collapsed, so unlike the old stories I'd heard—and the earthquake I'd survived in Haszen. The horse shook off its feet and sauntered across the plaza, disappearing on the side, the cobblestones under the scaffolding dried in a heartbeat, the silence returned, though peaceful this time.

And a group of men drifted out of the shadows, dry as the hay on a warm autumn afternoon in Elternow. The peace flashed away, but we hadn't come this far to be trapped in Windersay now. I stepped in front of Laurent, but he only kissed my cheek and called out toward them.

"Cadaval," he said, his voice stronger than I'd heard it in a long time. "Would you be kind enough to cut these ropes, please? It seems my wife can summon enchanted water but not a sword."

Laurent was silent as I placed another rag full of peppermint on his torn back, but I could tell I was causing him even more pain. His jaw worked back and forth as I dumped another handful of leaves into the bucket next to me, so I worked quicker, tossing the occasional order over my shoulder to the soldiers in worn leather breeches and the clean shirts of Vassian peasants who lingered in the room of the inn a few blocks away from the main square.

Willow bark, whiskey, boiling water—nothing I requested was denied, though I recoiled each time the door opened, expecting more of Damir's soldiers instead of Laurent's. Eventually, having satisfied themselves their king would live another day, the soldiers departed, minus Cadaval, who watched me minister to Laurent with the eyes of a wary, beaten dog.

"You can trust me," I finally snapped. "I didn't save him to murder him."

"Of course, Your Grace." He glanced backward at the bucket of water on the fire. "But someone should remain in case you need anything else."

"I don't know who you are, but I can tell you're hardly a servant." I dumped the last bloody rag in the bucket and stared at Laurent's back. He hadn't attended to me like this the night of our wedding, and though I would have never left him here to suffer alone, I wished he hadn't done so to me. "I don't believe waiting on us is what you're here for."

Laurent sighed. "Captain Cadaval has

been at my side since we left Lochfeld. I doubt even an order from me would shake his protection now. Not from you—but you can't forget we haven't made our way back to Meirdre yet."

"By your side the entire time, was he? It seems like you shook his protection yourself long enough to get yourself captured." My voice broke, and it wasn't from homesickness.

"Riette." His rebuke was quiet, but I knew I'd gone too far. "There are things—"

"I know." I settled back on my heels and basked in the fire's warmth. I was truly too stiff to sit like this, but I couldn't force myself farther away from him. "You had to get yourself and a small raiding party past the Vassian border. As a captive you could do so with much less bloodshed than an all-out attack."

Laurent rolled to his side, grimaced, and fixed me with a wary expression. Behind me, embers crackled as Cadaval stoked the fire.

"When we neared the Illrus River," he replied, "the scouts returned with unwelcome news—the Vassian Army was assembling at their outpost near Edrista, just like we'd feared. It was only days until they crossed the border, if that, and once that happened, they'd have flattened Meirdre as they proceeded north. So, I decided. If it was my death Damir wanted, he would get it—or at least, I'd let him think he would. We already knew Vassian had their own scouts heading toward Brannitz, so it was a straightforward matter to separate from the rest of the army and find them. Cadaval thought I was an idiot, I might add."

"I did, sire." Cadaval coughed, and a flash of pity rushed through me. Reporting directly to Laurent like he did must be as exasperating as being married to him. "And might have said as much to the stars when you retired to bed that night."

Laurent's eyes crinkled. "And now, Captain?"

"I suppose you were right, sire." A small smile broke through.

"But they—Thomas—suspected nothing when they found you?" I asked as Laurent's laugh faded. "You riding off on your own?"

Laurent forced a smile. "Perhaps a little. But they didn't question their good fortune. Of course, at that point I realized I needed you as well, so I convinced them they'd have to bring me to Lochfeld first. I said I knew Damir wanted you as well, but that you'd never go with them, however unwillingly, if you thought I was dead. Naturally they argued with me when I told them—they were certain I was lying, so I told them your secret. After that, they couldn't risk not believing me."

"But you could have told them anything else but that!"

"Hardly. You'd never have been able to hide your confusion if Thomas Wennink would have accused you of being anything but a crownkeeper. Telling the truth saved both our lives."

I swiveled my head toward Cadaval, but he must have known my secret, for he didn't look remotely shocked at the word. Though I suppose if he hadn't, my feat in the plaza would have erased all doubt. I turned back to Laurent, and tears filled my eyes. The image of him kneeling on the floor of the throne room, a sword at his throat . . . it would never leave my imagination, grand plan or not.

"I am sorry I frightened you." Laurent reached out a finger and brushed a tear from my cheek. "But I knew he would never hurt you without Damir's permission, and I knew—"

"You knew Damir couldn't hurt you as long as I wished otherwise." There. It was said. The accusation I'd been wanting to make since I'd realized why Laurent wasn't afraid. "As long as I fulfilled my duties."

He nodded.

"Why didn't you ever tell me what else I'm capable of?" I asked. "That water—the way it simply ran through the streets without harming anything—I've never seen anything like it. It's frightening to think I did that."

He stared at me, then rolled to his stomach once more.

"I didn't know until not that long ago. The map—yes, my father told me about that when I was a child, just after I first received the lecture regarding my duty to marry and produce heirs. But the other magic, the more secret magic, I didn't know about *that* until Father Gerritt told me just before I left Lochfeld. And even then, I wasn't certain how it could manifest—just that it would."

"I felt it." I lay my cheek on my hand, acutely conscious of our bystander. "On the ship. I tried to throw myself overboard, but before I could, we hit a wave. Out of nowhere, the sea turned from glass to something I can't even describe. It was terrifying. To know that *something* wanted me alive that badly . . ."

"You did promise you'd protect Lochfeld. And Meirdre. And me." Warmth filled his reminder. "The map—or more precisely, its magic—wasn't going to let you get away that easily."

"I suppose not." I took in a deep breath. "I need to refill the water."

Cadaval jumped to his feet. "Please, Your Grace, allow me."

"As I said, you're not a servant—and I'd be more comfortable if he had you here watching over him. I'll be fine." I brushed my fingers over Laurent's. "It's not as though I've never hauled water before."

Laurent raised his brows at my argument, and Cadaval nodded, so I grabbed the bucket and headed downstairs, swinging it from my hand. There was a pump out the back in the alleyway—I'd seen it when we'd come in— and the fresh air was calling me like it hadn't in a long while. It would be safe enough. While some of the villagers had trickled back into town, drawn by the stories of the wave that had destroyed nothing, most of the rest were still hiding in the cliffs, too fearful of a recurrence to chance coming home quite yet.

A few of the Meirdrean soldiers I recognized from upstairs glanced my way and nodded respectfully, but even my presence wasn't enough to tear them away from their well-deserved meat and ale. I slipped out the door, leaned against the wall, and took a deep breath of night air tinged with smoke from the surrounding chimneys. The stars were bright, and even if I was viewing them from a small village somewhere in Vassian, they looked almost the same as I'd seen every night in Elternow. And when I closed my eyes . . . I could almost believe I was still there. Except the scent of the peppermint and whiskey I'd used on Laurent's wounds wafted up from my hands, and my lips still stung with the taste of his. No, this was definitely not Elternow—it was something much better.

With a sigh of longing, I opened my eyes and trudged toward the pump. A shadowy figure turned the corner as I moved off the wall, and I stopped, the hair at the back of my neck prickling. Maybe we didn't need more water. Maybe Captain Cadaval or one of his men could get it. I shouldn't have felt afraid—it was evening, and the air was cool, so the figure's cloak wasn't out of place—but even so, I turned on my heel and headed for the back door of the inn where dozens of Meirdrean were waiting.

Just a few steps to safety . . .

A hand clamped over my mouth; the other shoved something hard and sharp against my side. The breeze turned cold as I tried to reconcile the sensation with the elation I'd felt just a few hours before, but I could feel nothing but heat. I gasped, and the pistol pushed harder.

"Hello, Riette," Thomas said.

CHAPTER THIRTEEN

Thomas pushed me against the wall with his knee, his palm still over my mouth and the pistol pressed against my stays. I gagged at the taste of the sweat on his palm, then swallowed enough of my fear to stop fighting him. It wasn't as though I could overpower him, and I didn't want that gun any closer to me than it already was.

"You're smarter than I thought. And more powerful." His fingers eased up on their pressure, just enough that I could breathe again. "Now, we're going to discuss our next steps. Don't move and don't scream."

"They'll come looking for me," I tried to mumble through his hand. "Soon."

"Unlikely." He flipped me around, my back against the wall, and leaned toward my ear. "If you were stupid enough to scream, you'd have done it already, not that there are many people left to hear you, thanks to that grandiose display of yours back at the plaza. Besides, those Meirdrean soldiers in there are too concerned with their ale to realize you left and didn't return."

"Who—"

"Oh, please." Thomas cackled. "They stick out. I don't know what your sovereign has planned, but if he thinks he's going to escape back across the border with less than twenty men, he's wrong."

The heat that insisted on filling my gut turned to ice. I didn't know what Laurent had planned, but Thomas was right. Any strategy he could have come up with on his way to Vassian would likely be futile.

Or would it? He'd intentionally let himself be captured by Vassian troops, after all. He couldn't be planning to take an entire kingdom with the men who'd made their way across the river, singly and in pairs, so he *must* have had a plan. If only he'd suggested it to me before I'd come downstairs.

I shook my head. "I don't know his plan either."

A slim figure, shrouded in shadows, caught my eye. I held my breath as it slipped around the corner and seemed to stop to watch me. It was entirely possible a bullet would end up in my side if he was startled by a resident out for a late evening walk.

"That doesn't surprise me." Thomas's lip curled—it was obvious he was unaware of our audience in the shadows. "Did you really think he'd mention it to *you*? A peasant girl from Elternow, who he refused to make his queen?"

I licked my lips as the slight wormed its way into my soul. The fact was, Laurent had said nothing to me. I hadn't questioned it before, but why should I? He had soldiers with him. I was only here to keep him alive, and I would have done that regardless of his intentions.

"His Majesty's military strategy is of little consequence to me, anyway," I whispered.

He laughed as he jerked me from the wall. "You can't lie to me, Riette. Never could. What girl wouldn't want more than he's given you? Especially now. You must already be wondering how much he truly appreciates your power. Or maybe he only appreciates you for your power—you can't believe he respects you, as much as he's kept you in the dark like he has."

With a shake of my head, I tried to twist from Thomas's grip, but he gave a jab of the pistol as he pulled me down the alley. A few Vassian women stepped outside to dump the remains of cooking water outside, but no one said a word—and I wasn't going to beg one of them for help. No, I would have to wait until I had a chance at overwhelming Thomas, before he could bring me somewhere from which I would never escape. The inn faded into the distance, but footsteps behind us grew louder.

"Riette?"

Thomas and I both froze. Well, he froze, then shoved the gun against me so hard I gasped, then spun me around to face our follower. I squinted at her—for the voice was undeniably feminine—but the moon had set, and she was hidden in the shadows.

"You have the wrong person," Thomas growled. "Now leave us, before you regret it."

"I think it's you that has the wrong person, Thomas Wennink."

My breath caught.

Oh, heavens.

Elsanne?

There was no way Laurent's mother could be standing here in a dark alley in Windersay, in the Kingdom of Vassian, but she'd been at Lochfeld long enough that I knew her voice, and now, the familiar posture of a woman who'd long ceased to fear anyone like Thomas. Did she have a sword under that cape? Probably. Knowing Elsanne, it might even be a musket.

Thomas jerked me closer to him. I swung my free hand at him, momentarily forgetting the pistol. He must have done the same, for when he reached out to catch my wrist, the gun clattered to the cobblestones. I kicked it away as he grabbed me, catching my shoe in my skirts and tripping backward, away from him.

Elsanne's shadow grew larger in the dim alley, and before I could find my feet, she'd yanked me back into a doorway behind us.

Finally, I scrambled up, searching for the pistol somewhere out on the darkened stones, but there was no use. Thomas gave us one last look and took off north, giving me only a brief glance over his shoulder as he sprinted.

She turned to me and put a cool hand to my cheek. "Are you injured?"

For a moment I could only stare, trying to figure out if I was imagining her. Was this another of Laurent's games? Not likely, I decided. No matter what it gained him, Laurent would never involve his mother in something like this.

"No—he didn't hurt me."

"Surprising, given how poorly you fight." Her eyes glistened in the shadows as she focused on me. "And where might my son be?"

I gawked at her. "An inn."

"Well? Are you going to take me there or just stand here?"

"I—yes, of course, Your Majesty."

I skulked back into the alley and led her toward the inn where I hoped Laurent was still waiting safely, the hair still standing on the back of my neck. Though desperate to know how and why Elsanne was here alone —and how she'd found me—I didn't dare question her after she'd asked for Laurent in that tone. I didn't even dare to fill the bucket I'd left near the pump when Thomas had grabbed me. Cadaval could do so, since he'd been so motivated before. Maybe he could take Elsanne with him, for I wasn't sure I wanted to see how Laurent was going to react to her appearance—or the fact Thomas had grabbed me.

Four soldiers meandered about the hallway outside Laurent's door when I climbed the stairs, and I didn't look any of them in the eye as I slid inside and approached the bed. Laurent's eyes were closed, a blanket pulled up over his bare chest, and I placed a hand on his, ignoring

Cadaval's critical expression. He could try telling Elsanne she couldn't enter if he felt like it.

"Sire? There's—there's someone here to see you."

He brushed his fingers over mine, smiled, then cracked one eye.

"She made it, did she?"

"Indeed I did," Elsanne broke in before I could formulate any kind of stunned reply. "Only to find Riette here being dragged off by that Wennink creature. All these soldiers milling about, and you couldn't assign one to protect your wife? What were you thinking, Laurent?"

Laurent sat bolt upright, a man on his throne instead of a dirty bed in a foreign inn.

"She what?" he asked, his eyes landing on mine.

"When I went to get the water." I collapsed in the nearest chair and placed a palm where Thomas's pistol had been. "He was right there. Like he was waiting for me. He—they've returned to the village. They must be watching the inn. Why they haven't yet barged in here, I can't begin to imagine."

Laurent snapped his fingers, and two of the soldiers who'd followed Elsanne and me inside vanished out the door. "And then?"

"She tried to hit him when I showed up." Elsanne's voice dripped something. Not scorn, but certainly not approval. "And he ran."

"To Damir, most likely," Laurent replied. "And if he recognized you, he'll know exactly why you're here, and we won't have that much time. We must move quickly."

"Much time for what?" I asked foolishly.

My chest closed in, but I wasn't sure it was from the utter fatigue or Thomas's suggestions regarding my marriage. Maybe Thomas was right. Laurent had told his mother his plans but not me? Did he not trust me? Not love me? Not think me capable of acting as a crownkeeper? Or worse, his wife?

"Marius—" Laurent began. Cadaval shot him a sharp look, so he paused, glanced at Elsanne, and then back to me. "He's been leading his army toward Vassian since . . . well, for several weeks now, I would imagine. Ever since my mother used my departure from Lochfeld as an opportunity to run home to Iraela like I expressly ordered her not to."

Elsanne's mouth dropped open. "I—"

"Are predictable, Mother, yes." He winced as he shifted. I stood and moved toward him, but he waved me off. "And your arrival in Iraela was enough to tip off Marius that things had been set in motion, enough to let him send a rider to his men waiting in the wastes of the Coalwood Basin. Tobias Erstad is with them, in case you were wondering," he said to me. "Vahl's men chased him out of Meirdre, and he stumbled across Marius's army, terrified he'd fated you to death. I'll let you apologize."

A shudder of relief ran through me. I'd long believed Erstad dead.

"As for Marius," Laurent went on, "I may owe him the next seven generations of my children, but at least Meirdre will be safe—and I'll have cemented an alliance with Iraela as well. Properly this time. Splitting a conquered kingdom between each other tends to do that."

I straightened in my chair and stared at him. "You mean to say—"

"That we intend on taking Vassian?" Laurent gave me a brilliant smile. "Yes. We unlocked the door. Marius and the Iraelan Army will knock it down."

CHAPTER FOURTEEN

THE ROOM GREW SILENT. ELSANNE STARED AT Laurent, her lip twisted in a disappointed expression—but even she knew to be silent when her son had made such a declaration. Me, I had no such restraint, not anymore. If Laurent wanted to reprimand me, at least now he knew exactly *who* he was reprimanding—a crownkeeper who'd just proven she could control the tides.

"You don't mean that," I breathed out.

Cadaval cleared his throat.

Laurent's brows rose. "What part of this plan was confusing for you, my dear?"

"None of it, sire. I only . . ." I stopped, finally aware of my foolishness. "But where is King Marius? If he'd been here, I wouldn't have had to—do what I did."

Laurent shrugged, casually, like I hadn't just saved him from further whipping and death. "He's heading this way, I would imagine. Round south the Bolcour Mountains or taking care of that stronghold at Edrista first, I have no idea, but they'll be here, and soon."

"You said *unlock the door*," I began hesitantly. "What exactly did you mean?"

His smile fell. "The plan was for Damir to let his guard down a bit at the border once he had me. Makes Marius's job of passing through the Basin easier—our own soldiers following behind as well. But it seems he was too impatient for my death—that's changed the timeline a bit, as you've probably figured out. We've bought ourselves tonight, after what you did in the plaza, but after that, we're going to have to come up with something different."

"And Thomas. He found me and he'll know you're close by." My heart began to pound again. "It won't be long until they find you."

"Likely." Laurent glanced up, as if he'd just remembered Cadaval and his mother were still in the room. "I need to speak with Riette alone, please."

Cadaval simply nodded as he disappeared out the door, but Elsanne straightened.

"You used me." Her tone was low with fury. "Once more. I should—"

Laurent sighed, cutting her off. "I am righting a wrong, Mother. One I was partially responsible in creating."

"You were thoughtless," she snapped back at him. "And now you've wrapped two kingdoms up in your careless plot."

"You'd prefer to kneel to Damir?" It sounded like a threat that should have been shouted, but Laurent's voice was terrifyingly even. "Because you would, eventually. Yes, even with Marius's army. You know Vassian won't stop at Meirdre, especially with us having the most tenuous connections to another kingdom. I did what I had to do, and Marius agreed. If this all ends poorly, it ends poorly, but history will not accuse me of not doing everything I could to protect my land and people after so foolishly doing the opposite before."

I swallowed at his mention of the bargain with Iraela. Elsanne gave a small huff, no doubt annoyed at the reminder of being sold as a hostage as well.

"Do you trust me?" he asked. "Do you trust Marius? You travelled all the way here on his order after all—alone, no less—apparently knowing very little of why he commanded it of you."

"I try." Her shoulders sagged, making her look less like a queen in costly traveling clothes and more like a woman accepting the inevitable. "But this plan of yours is difficult to trust."

"Your loyalty will not be in vain." He struggled to his feet and gave her a quick kiss on each cheek. "I promise you that, Mother."

"Then I will not question you again." She cupped her hand on his jaw, and I suddenly saw him as the beloved child he must have been at one time. "But this had better be the last time I fall into one of your plans. Next time I will not be so understanding, sire."

Regardless of her words, I doubted Laurent had seen the last of her, but she disappeared into the hall with a respectful nod. I threw a cautious glance at the door, then guided him back to bed.

"I would never have said it in front of my mother, or even Cadaval, but things happened too quickly," he said, collapsing. "Fool

I might have been, but I didn't realize Damir was so eager for my death." He angled toward me, and I leaned against his chest, avoiding several whip marks. "I doubt Marius is as near to Windersay as he should be at this point. And now that Wennink knows where I am—there are precious few places we can hide until the Army of Iraela arrives."

"And Vassian soldiers are protecting the Meirdrean border, no doubt." I reached for another rag, but he waved me off.

"There is no going home now." He sighed once more. "Not yet."

"So, we need to delay." I matched his sigh with a deep exhale of my own. "For how long?"

Laurent ran a hand through his hair. "A week, possibly."

Heavens. A week. He was wrong. He had to be. I doubted we had another day in this inn.

"You must have an idea," I replied. "You wouldn't have said anything to me if you didn't."

He reached for a glass of water by the bedside and drained it in one gulp. "A few bad ones," he admitted. "Cadaval suspects the direness of our circumstances. He wants me to make a run for it, but I won't leave my men—or you. And I fear our other options are similarly poor. Make no mistake, this is not the end, but things have become rather complicated."

I stared at the floor for a long while. A tower flashed into my mind, a stone window and the feel of the ocean breeze on my skin, a too-recent memory I'd rather have forgotten. But could it be the answer? I didn't want to broach the subject, but Laurent almost seemed to be asking for my thoughts. And mine was certainly better than Cadaval's ideas of running, well-intentioned though it was.

"Damir still wants me," I said quietly. "I'm sure of it. When the water came, he was watching me as I stood, and he wasn't surprised by what was happening in the least. I don't believe he expected the water, but he expected *something*. He wants my power for himself, and badly. My appearance would startle enough to distract him from his plans for you."

"No." If it was possible after his whipping, Laurent's face paled even more. "I know what I said before, but now—I forbid it."

"Do you have a better solution?" My mouth was dry with fear, but I pressed on. "He was desperate to see if a crownkeeper's power will work outside of Meirdre. Now he knows—the only question remaining in his mind is if he can make it work for him."

"It could work." He stood and paced to the far wall before dropping on the bed again. Blood seeped through the bandages, but I knew better than to tell him to rest. I watched him instead, trying to decipher his expression, but his face was stone. "But I will not permit it."

"But sire—"

"I will not risk your life like that."

I ran a finger down his jaw. "Isn't my life already at risk?"

"It is." Laurent turned my face toward his and leaned against me, cheek to cheek. He was silent for a long time. "And because of that, I'm inclined to let you do this, however ill-advised it may seem. But I must ask you one thing . . . is it Thomas Wennink you want? Is that what this is about?"

For a moment I thought he had slapped me, such was the heat that passed over my cheeks before taking over my entire body.

"Sire, I would never—"

"Perhaps not. But I wouldn't be a man if I didn't question it." There wasn't anger in the statement, not even an accusation. Fear? Yes, some of that. Fear and desperation. And I understood. I hadn't ever truly loved Thomas, but I couldn't blame Laurent for wondering. Especially not now. "Especially since you left with him once before," he added.

Tears filled my eyes at his decidedly unregal fear. I had been stupid, naïve, untrusting. Had hurt a man who'd only wanted a loving marriage. Was it any wonder he was worried about my intentions now?

"I love you." The words were so easy to say now. "No one else. Ever."

"Prove it." His voice grew husky. "And once we return to Meirdre, you will wear the crown that started this all."

"I don't care about the crown." I shifted toward him, suddenly frantic for his touch. "Just you."

His command wasn't a challenge, I knew. More of a desperation to love me like he hadn't been able to bring himself to do the night of our wedding. He pulled me onto his lap with only the slightest flinch. The fire crackled as he drew my dress over my head, and he didn't speak as my lips lingered on his, promising something unsaid, something too insistent to be uttered with words. I shrank back then, wordless and afraid of his wounds, but he gripped me so fiercely that I almost forgot to breathe as I gave in to desire —though I wasn't sure which one of us needed and wanted it more. I'd meant to reassure him, but he'd ended up comforting me.

Still, I knew, while I watched his chest rise and fall in exhausted slumber afterward, that when he woke, all those reassurances would mean nothing.

CHAPTER FIFTEEN

THE BACKSTREETS OF WINDERSAY WERE silent when I slipped along a row of houses several hours later. Even the wharf was quiet, though a sailor who'd been brave enough to return was singing somewhere in the distance, a melody of homesickness and loss. I had stopped shivering once I turned and the buildings blocked the wind, but I still shook as I hurried along, turning backward every so often to check for pursuers. Nothing could block the fear.

Nothing could block my feeling of failure, either. I'd been wandering around the village for almost a half hour now, and surely someone would have seen me by now. Surely someone would have recognized me as the woman who'd summoned water to rescue the king of Meirdre, and they wouldn't hesitate to turn me back over to Damir. I certainly didn't want to show up at the front gate of his clifftop fortress. Confused and angry was the plan, not immediate surrender.

Even so, I turned west, toward the colossal tower that loomed over the thatched roofs and sails. The soldiers would be more numerous the closer I got to the fortress, and perhaps Damir wouldn't question it. A scorned woman, wandering in circles, trying to decide if she *was* going to commit treason tonight . . . yes. And Thomas, finally useful, could confirm that yes, *Riette has a tendency to abandon her duties, run off and follow her childish emotions. Even when they lead to treachery.*

The idea of seeing him again made my stomach churn, so I focused on the cobblestones I'd walked just hours before, so certain I would witness Laurent's death. He'd made it out of that, hadn't he? Without me knowing the extent of my crownkeeper abilities, no less. Not that I was certain I knew the full extent now—what else was the magic hiding from me? I didn't feel it now, but perhaps that meant nothing. I'd felt nothing but despair watching Laurent ride down the hill in that wagon, after all—until I hadn't.

I mused over that as two Vassian soldiers passed me by. They looked me up and down, but their interest appeared personal instead of professional. That alone was enough to set my hair on edge once more. I quickened my step, trying to decide how I would explain to Damir that I'd passed up several of his soldiers before deciding to surrender. But no matter how suspicious that was, I couldn't turn around and speak to them now without them asking questions themselves.

Lights and voices inside an inn ahead caught my eyes. Early morning it might be, but at least some residents of Windersay were still up—likely ones who were celebrating their survival and drowning in ale their sorrows over Laurent's escape, I hoped. Just . . . just not *too* much ale. I crept closer to peek inside, staying in the shadows of the alley. The magic, I hoped, would tell me if this was the place to make my appearance. It was difficult to tell through the fogged-over window, but it appeared most of the patrons were sailors and workers from the docks— though a few soldiers were visible in the corner, their uniforms obvious through the condensation dripping down the glass.

"What's this?"

I started at the voice. It was a tavern worker who'd caught me staring.

"You look familiar." He peered at me through the shadows, and I held my breath. "That Meirdrean girl! The one who—"

My legs acted without permission, and I darted toward the left, away from his grip. Suddenly, with my goal within reach, I was too terrified to follow through. I would have to run back to the inn, would have to find Laurent, confess my failure. He would forgive me, I was certain, but . . .

Would I forgive myself?

I froze at the internal question, my chest heaving. The man was beside me in two steps, and when his fingers curled around my upper arm, I didn't fight back. I didn't protest as he led me inside the tavern, my appearance stopping all conversation immediately. I had, apparently, found a group of Windersay residents who recognized me at once.

An officer in the corner rose, interest

written all over his face. "Where'd you find her, Leontiou?"

"Skulking around out back." He pushed me forward, into the center of the tavern. "Listening in who knows what. Probably trying to decide what dark magic to use on us next."

"I wasn't listening to anything," I replied, rubbing my wrists in a vain attempt to calm myself. "I couldn't have heard through the glass even if I wanted to."

"Then why are you here?" he asked.

I shook off the tavern owner's hand on my arm. "I have information for King Damir."

The room fell silent, except for the distant calls of birds, disturbed from their nightly slumber by the rising sun near the horizon.

"What kind of information?" The officer circled around me, as though he'd discover the information just by staring at me.

Looking through me. "Surely you can't expect me to disturb His Majesty on nothing more than your word."

"That"—I lifted my chin, if only to convince myself of my non-existent bravery—"is only for King Damir's ears. If you know who I am, you will not risk arguing with me."

A roar of laughter. It filled my mind, along with a certain sense of purpose I'd been missing since Thomas had pushed me onto that ship way back in Vistel. And suddenly, somewhere deep inside me, I realized Laurent and I had made the right decision by allowing this foolish endeavor. The map? Some other magic? My own soul, letting me know I was *finally* doing something right? Maybe it didn't matter.

"Then by all means," the officer said, gesturing me toward the front door, "let's get you to King Damir."

In the early morning darkness, the tower I thought I'd never see again was cold, even with the window closed. I paced from it to the door and back, sometimes counting my steps, sometimes simply walking, my mind elsewhere. Was it fear? There was some of that threatening to bubble up, but also a certain giddiness—Damir no doubt knew I'd turned myself in, which meant Laurent was safe for now. And the longer he waited to see me, the longer it took for him to debate my intentions and power, the closer King Marius and his army would be to Windersay.

A flicker of gilded sunlight appeared through the window as the sun rose, and I yawned despite myself. Sleep was tempting, but I knew I'd dream of Laurent if I could find a comfortable position on the stone floor, so I continued my pacing. No one came, not Damir, nor Thomas, nor any of the soldiers, and by the time the sun set once more, my stomach was growling.

But that was one much-needed day down. One day to allow Laurent to heal. To allow King Marius's approach. Or had Damir ignored my message totally? Had he headed back into Windersay, searching each inn and private home for Laurent?

My eyes burned as I leaned against the wall and let my imagination take control. It was difficult to dream with the smell of salt on the breeze, but if I concentrated, I could feel Laurent's hands on my skin. The earthy scent of horses in the Lochfeld stables. The breeze through the apple orchards outside Elternow. Would I live to experience them? Would Meirdre exist in another month? All of it was too much to think about, so I stood on the stone bench and tried to yank the window shut. It would make the tower room claustrophobic, but if I could only ignore the perfume of the sea, perhaps I could ignore the entire situation—especially since the door creaked open just as I hopped down.

"Are you planning on jumping?" Damir asked, closing the door behind him.

"I hate the smell of the ocean," I replied. "It smells . . . rotten."

"I doubt that, after what I witnessed last night." He gave me a sullen smile. "You told my soldiers you had something to tell me?"

I took a breath. It would be the most difficult lie I'd ever told, and yet the most important. But the shadows of the tower embraced me as I swallowed, calming me somehow. Like they know my motive and were holding me in their own approval.

"I was wrong," I said, keeping my voice soft. Disappointed. Not distraught, for I doubted Damir would listen to a distraught woman, no matter what information or powers she held. "Wrong to do it, wrong to run afterward. Because even after what I did, he—he didn't want me after all."

His eyes widened a fraction. "And you're angry."

Tears wet my cheeks, so easy. "I sacrificed so much for him, and he threw it all away, all because he was afraid of my gifts."

Damir sank to the bench opposite me, half shrouded in darkness, half shimmering in the moonlight. Dusky circles under his eyes shadowed his expression, but the lines in his face had faded somewhat, like my appearance had been the answer to his prayers. A moonbeam hit the clasps on his cloak as he shifted, and a pair of dragons stared back at me, disappearing into the shadows as he leaned against the wall.

"I would not be," he replied. "The power you showed last night is not to be discarded out of fear. Any sovereign worth anything would see that."

"I thought you might understand." I looked out the window, like I was second-guessing my decision. Rushing would seem suspicious. In truth, I was searching for wherever Laurent might be, praying he might send me some of his strength some-how. Was that silly? It felt like it, but some-thing told me Laurent wouldn't mind sharing. Not now. "And that means you de-serve the power. Vassian deserves it."

"Then you confess that you lied to me be-fore. That you do have powers. And you were well aware of them when we last spoke."

"I wouldn't think I'd need to confess after what happened down in the village." I gave him a choked laugh, one I didn't need to feign. "But no. Until last night, I wasn't aware that what I did there was possible. It surprised me as much as it must have sur-prised you."

"Hmm."

He studied me so long that the glint of moonlight drifted across the floor. Time was both my friend and enemy—the longer I sat here, the closer I was to losing my nerve, but the more chance Laurent and King Marius had of seeing things through. The very idea made me shake, the responsibility too heavy to bear.

"Then we shall see what else you are capable of," he said, slapping his palms on the bench. "But not here."

"Not here?" I stammered.

He smiled and pointed toward the door. "Not here."

CHAPTER SIXTEEN

THE CARRIAGE DAMIR SHOWED ME TO WAS AS unlike the cart in which Laurent had ridden as possible. Though I hated to admit it, it could have been called more luxurious than the one in which I'd ridden to Iraela so long ago. If only I didn't have to share with Damir and Thomas, it could have been . . . almost enjoyable.

But Thomas's sneer had grown old long before we'd settled into our journey on the road from Windersay to Damir's principal palace outside Heosta. I couldn't help but wonder if he knew my true motivation for being here, but he hadn't said anything to Damir yet, so I had to assume I was safe—for a while, at least. I leaned my head against the side as Damir made small talk with me about the spring planting season, and I tried to ignore his voice as the sun came up and filled the carriage with an unwelcome warmth.

He had claimed, when we'd departed the tower, that the trip to the palace would take less than two days. By the way the driver was whipping the horses, I believed it. Still, I couldn't help wishing he'd urge them on faster, if only because I couldn't stand the idea of spending the night in a strange inn in Vassian, Thomas in a nearby room. But we came to a stop as the sun dipped low in the distance, outside a squat building built around what looked like a courtyard. Strange trees surrounded it—plain, brown trunks with a set of fanlike leaves on top. I'd never seen such a thing except in books, and despite Thomas's presence, I couldn't help staring at the exotic sight.

Damir jumped out of the carriage into the sand below, all silk and fine leather and unnecessary bluster toward the innkeeper, and I pressed myself into the velvet seat, hoping he would forget about me. But he motioned me out, Thomas at my side, and I trudged upstairs to a small, spartan room. The cracked window overlooked the road, enough that I could see anyone coming to my rescue.

But that was silly, for there was no rescue coming. I'd volunteered for this, hadn't I? And I was succeeding—I'd tempted Damir away from Windersay. It was a waiting game now.

"We leave early in the morning for Heosta," Thomas said before shutting the door. "Don't do anything stupid."

I ignored him and deadbolted the door. Despite the dust from the road that needed to wash off, I curled up on the ancient bed, still in my stays and gown, and stifled a yawn as it creaked. I wanted Laurent's arms around me, and I wanted to go home, so I closed my eyes and let sleep take me. If I couldn't see either right now, at least I could see both in my dreams.

I woke to the sliding of the deadbolt on the inside of my door. I must have dreamed the intrusion before it woke me, for my heart was already pounding. I told myself it was simply Thomas come to wake me up to resume my journey—not that I approved of that familiarity of him entering my room at all, but it would have been a *reason*—but moonlight still cascaded across the floor when I opened my eyes and tried to focus in the darkness.

It wasn't Thomas who'd entered, though.

Damir stood there in the moonlight, but I could tell in an instant that his intentions were . . . well, not noble, but also not what I'd initially feared. The curiosity was simply too plain on his face.

"What do you want?" I clutched the blanket to my chest as he stood there, staring.

"I couldn't wait until we reach Heosta to see what else your powers allow." He took a step toward me. "I have to know now. Please."

The desperation in his *please* threw me. Laurent had sounded that desperate once, back when I had thought little of him. Could Damir possibly have some compelling reason for wanting access to my powers?

I shook off the question. Pity was the last thing I needed to feel for him now. Even if the dragons of old themselves were raiding Vassian, his fate was not my business. Damir would deserve his scorched farmland, and even as a farmer's daughter, I would be happy enough to watch.

"It's the middle of the night," I replied, drawing up my most regal tone, "and I would have assumed to be treated with more propriety than this. You couldn't have waited until the morning, at least?"

He shook his head and took another step forward. I sighed and swung my feet to the floor. Maybe it didn't matter. There was no magic floating through the inn that I could sense, so he was likely only wasting his time and my sleep. I padded along next to him as he led me to the courtyard, brighter than I would have expected in the moonlight. The fountain in the center bubbled as we entered, and I sank to the edge, letting the cool water flow over my fingers. Now that the time had come, it scarcely calmed the heat I felt in my soul.

"What exactly are you expecting from me?" I asked.

"I saw you call for the water, even if you didn't know what you were doing." He circled the fountain, his gaze never leaving mine. "Perhaps something with the fountain. What do you think? Is it calling to you?"

I jerked my fingers out of the water and wiped them on my skirts. Finally, it had to come to this. I had known when I'd left Laurent in Windersay that I was taking a risk—that he might not catch up to me once Damir's soldiers had vacated the town, leaving Laurent safe. Nausea rolled through my gut. Damir was seconds from calling my bluff, and once he did—

"I don't feel anything," I said. "Maybe if you were in danger, I might. We should continue on the road to Heosta and see if anything changes." Fear prickled a warning in my gut, but I couldn't help issuing him an order. "If there are bandits, or a flood, or even a sandstorm, then perhaps that would put you in enough danger to—"

"I may be desperate for your power, but I am not a fool," he interrupted. His leathery face smooth in the moonlight as he peered at me, then shouted over his shoulder, words I didn't understand until three soldiers appeared in the shadows behind him. "I think you've been playing me, and now I want the truth."

Fear.

I might not feel the magic that had sometimes inundated Lochfeld, but I felt raw fear now. It was the only thing I could sense, actually, and as the soldiers came closer, I made my decision. I'd saved Laurent this time, hadn't I? If I died, he would be forced to remarry, and perhaps it wouldn't matter if his next wife was a crownkeeper or not. Perhaps I'd only been fated to meet him to save his life in Windersay.

"I told Thomas the magic is limited to Lochfeld," I whispered to my feet, "and I thought I had spoken the truth. But I was wrong. It's the Kingdom of Meirdre it protects. Meirdre and her sovereign. I cannot serve you, even if I wished." I lifted my head and met his stare. "And I do not wish."

If he felt rage, I couldn't see it in his expression.

"I see," he replied, his voice level. "So, you have betrayed me."

I knew I should stop talking before I made things worse. But then, could there possibly be a worse situation than the one I was currently in? I wasn't escaping, that much was certain, and that meant—that meant Damir needed to know exactly how I felt about him.

I steadied my feet. "My loyalty was never to you, sir."

For a long while, he said nothing.

"No? I suppose I should have expected nothing less from a Meirdrean peasant girl." His lips twisted in a sort of cruel smile. "You have made your decision. You shall die as your husband should have."

Before I could imagine how that would be, the soldiers grabbed me and flung me to my knees in front of the fountain. I screamed and kicked and tried to stand, but they spread my arms to my sides and held me, throat-first, against the stone. My fingertips clawed against the stone, but their weight and the position in which they held me was too powerful to fight. Images of the night the executioner had chained me to the whipping block in the dungeon of Lochfeld flooded my mind, but this time—this time I wouldn't survive.

Damir pushed my hair to the side and stroked the back of my neck with his palm as he knelt beside me.

"Laurent is in pursuit, no doubt," he whispered into my ear, drawing a chill down my spine. "And I will be kind enough to let him find your body here. Give him something to bring back to Meirdre and mourn—do not think I cannot show some mercy to him. Maybe, if he searches long enough, he might even find your head as well."

I choked down a cry as the surrounding darkness grew. It didn't make sense. The moon hadn't set yesterday until well into the morning, which meant it shouldn't be gone now, so soon before sunrise. Was this what sheer terror did to a soul?

A breeze brushed over my skin as he stood and unsheathed his sword. I pressed my mouth against the stone to hide my sobs and closed my eyes as the shadows turned to a glittering gold brilliance. Finally, there was the sunrise that I'd prayed would bring hope. Moonlight or not, I wouldn't die in darkness at least, and that was something. Executed on a clear night was a traitor's death at home. Dying in the light, that I could handle. Laurent would be relieved when he learned how it had happened. He would understand what it meant to me—and to him.

"What is it they say in Meirdre?" Damir asked. "Godspeed into eternity? Well, it'll have to do."

It wasn't what they said in the least, but I could scarcely remember what they *did* say, for the sun's heat on my back had turned to fire as he spoke. I flinched into the stone, more at the hope welling up than at the sword I knew he'd raised above his head. I opened my eyes, and my breath caught at the familiar shimmering glow that bathed the courtyard in light.

The sword whistled through the air.

I tensed as my teeth slid against each other, my muscles so painful that death would be a blessing. But it was shattered metal, cool and smooth and tiny, that fell against the back of my neck like rain. What didn't wind up tangled in my hair cascaded to the sand beside me. Glitter, like some of my visions had been. I turned my head to the side just as the hilt bounced harmlessly off my hip and landed on the ground. The glow faded as it did, leaving me with an aching head—but one which was still attached to my body.

Laurent had done this.

Tears welled up as I remembered those last hours in that room in Windersay. He'd promised to make me the queen of Meirdre, and his vow had saved me—for whatever magic flooded our kingdom now saw me as worthy of its protection as Laurent was. Had he known the power he was giving me when we said goodbye?

Damir backed toward the archway that led to the front of the inn, his right hand curled as though he still held the sword that lay in a million pieces next to the fountain. Eyes wide and wild, he muttered a prayer—or maybe a curse. I gasped for air, and then, finding my hands free, pulled myself to my feet with the help of the stone wall. I could barely move to defend myself, but the soldiers had already disappeared, too afraid, apparently, of the power I'd finally demonstrated.

The sun's rays crested the roof of the inn while Damir and I stared at each other, and as I shook off the headache, shouts and the whinnies of horses replaced the sound of my labored breathing. Outside the courtyard, figures hollered at both each other and nothingness. Laurent and his men? Or simply bandits who would kill all of us if they had the chance? Though I'd suggested it to Damir, I wasn't nearly educated enough about Vassian to know if there was a common threat on this road as it was in parts of Meirdre.

The shouts turned to musket shots. Bellowing for a new sword, Damir took off running. I backed to the other side of the fountain and slid to the ground, praying it hid me from whomever had arrived. If I was lucky, they would take what they wanted and simply head off down the road.

My eyes threatened to close out of sheer fatigue, but my heart refused to cooperate as I slumped over. A dreadful quiet overtook the courtyard, then the slamming of doors and windows overtook it. No voices joined the sound, so I pressed myself against the ground and dragged a finger through what remained of Damir's sword. The rising sun illuminated some of the courtyard but left the rest shrouded in deep shadows, enough that I hoped whoever had arrived would give up and go away before finding me—for I was now certain that it wasn't Laurent.

I lay motionless as the voice shouted for me, though I didn't know why. Whoever they were, they knew who I was and that I was here. Had they tortured someone for the information? There was no way to know. The one thing I did know was this: if it was one of Laurent's men, there was no threat. If it was one of Damir's men—or Thomas— well, how many times could I rely on that magic? Possibly an infinite amount, though I had no desire to test that prediction.

"Where the hell is that girl?" the voice continued when I didn't reply. "They said she was here in the inn—how hard could she possibly be to find? If I found out Damir's men lied—"

My heart skipped a beat. I tried to pull myself upright, but the headache hadn't faded in the least, and my strength seemed to have disappeared along with that dreadful sword. Not caring any longer how disheveled I appeared when they found me, I collapsed back into the sand and sobbed in relief.

It wasn't Damir coming back for me.
Or Thomas.
It was King Marius of Iraela.

CHAPTER SEVENTEEN

"Laurent is perhaps a half-day behind us," Marius told me as I leaned against the archway in the garden behind the inn. The rising sun cut through the early chill, so I didn't argue about his chosen place for this discussion. He hadn't removed his palm from the pommel of his sword since they'd found me behind the fountain, and I knew the anxiety of battle would take more than an hour to dissipate—especially since more was likely to come. "But his wounds are likely slowing him, so we will stay until he reaches us."

"And I appreciate that protection, my lord. But Damir—"

"Fled south toward Heosta. My men caught him before he reached the river. He should have not tried to make a stand there —the animals will take care of his body."

"And Thomas Wennink?" My knees shook as I spoke. I couldn't celebrate Damir's death, but I hadn't known relief could make one so weak.

"I don't know the name." He shrugged off my question. "Likely escaped with the rest of them who separated from Damir. None of them will get far."

I wasn't so certain about that, but I gave him a respectful nod and wandered back inside, intent on that bath I'd scorned last night. If nothing else, Laurent would appreciate the scent of clean skin instead of horse. The inn's owner and servants had gone missing as soon as the army of Iraela had appeared, so I lugged a few buckets of hot water into the washing room off the main kitchen and stripped my grimy clothing off. The only soap I could locate was cheap kitchen lye, but I ran it through my hair. It was better than nothing.

When I dressed in a new gown—pilfered from the carriage Damir had left—and reentered the kitchen, the soldiers who'd been filling their stomachs earlier were gone. I could see them outside in the courtyard, laughing and cleaning their swords and muskets. I couldn't help a smile at the ordinariness of it all, despite the shards of metal that still lay in the dust.

I began to hum as I dug through the cupboards for some spare bread, anything to stave off my growing hunger. Even though they'd run off, I was sure the owner and his staff would be back, and I didn't want to take much from them, even if they were Vassian.

Elternow was too recent in my memories, and I knew how sacred food could be in a remote place like this. Finding a pomegranate, I polished it with my skirt and headed to the courtyard to watch the soldiers spar with each other.

The rear stairwell creaked as I approached, and the hair on my arms stood up. It was likely nothing, just another soldier coming downstairs, but my chest grew tight as I backed into the kitchen, the only place I could think to hide. Marius's men made noise. They didn't slip silently around an inn they now controlled.

Footsteps resonated down the stairs and just outside the kitchen, and I gasped for air as they came closer.

As the fire behind me, untended for hours, gave a dying gasp.

As a gleeful shout echoed outside, an Iraelan battle cry of victory.

As Thomas slipped in the kitchen with a broad grin and a sword in his hand.

The apple fell to the floor.

"You'd best run, Thomas," I said, swallowing hard. "They will not treat you kindly if they find you in here. And they will."

"Unlikely." He glanced down at the sword, then back at me. "The fools are celebrating their success, too stupid to realize they've been too hasty in their festivities."

"And what? You think killing me will solve anything?" *If you're even able to.* "You think it will prevent Marius and his army from taking the castle at Heosta and making sure no one replaces Damir?"

"Maybe not." Thomas shrugged. "But solutions aren't my goal at this point—revenge is."

I backed against the stone wall, ash coating the bottom of my skirts. Thomas hadn't cared about Damir and Vassian after all. They were a means to an end.

"Your argument is with me," I said. "Not Laurent. Leave him out of it."

"It's with both of you." He took a step toward me. "You've taken everything from me."

"You didn't even want me," I whispered. I'd have shouted it, but I didn't trust him to not run me through with that sword if I let the soldiers outside hear me. "And he did!"

"And you didn't mind turning your back on Elternow, did you?"

Right before I died was a strange time to bring up my supposed sins, but I couldn't let him criticize that decision. I wouldn't let him speak of my marriage like that. And though I could be silent around Laurent when protocol demanded it of me, Thomas had earned no such respect.

"You turned your back on Elternow," I ground out. "I protected Mama and Papa, especially after you destroyed their home. I gave them a life. A future. I sacrificed everything to protect Meirdre!"

"It's hardly a sacrifice if you parade around Lochfeld in pretty gowns on the arm of a tyrant, is it?" He glanced at my current attire as he stepped even closer. "Though I suppose even a queen has to give up the pretty gowns and beg for charity eventually."

"I would back off if I were you, Thomas." I slid against the wall toward the fireplace, wondering if I could climb up the chimney. "Unless you want to see for yourself exactly what happened here earlier this morning. You do not want to cross Lochfeld's magic."

By the look on his face, I realized he *had* been there, somewhere in the background.

"Then maybe I won't try to kill you. Or maybe I'll wait until your power fades one day." His lip curled up. "Right now, I was more thinking I'd sample Laurent's goods before I destroy his life—I've always wondered what he saw in you. The fire pit isn't ideal, but it will do."

"Leave me alone," I whispered. "Go away and leave me alone."

He grinned. "I don't think I will."

"You will do what she says, Wennink."

Laurent's order echoed through the kitchen. Thomas spun around, but not before I caught the look of horror in his eyes. His sword fell a fraction, then his fingers went rigid on the grip. I didn't know which one of us was more surprised, but surprised or not, he clearly intended to fight.

"After all," Laurent continued, a smile playing about his lips, "she is the Queen of Meirdre. As such, you are subject to her commands."

Thomas scoffed. My eyes floated to Laurent's gaze, but he wasn't looking at me. His attention was solely on Thomas, and when Thomas lifted his sword, he took a graceful step backward, the picture of a swordsman who'd been accomplished since he was old enough to lift a weapon.

But I'd seen the whip marks on his back, knew how badly it must hurt to stretch his skin to heft a sword like he was. Thomas followed him out the door, and though Laurent didn't stumble, his smile faded as he steadied himself on the wood floor of the main room.

"You've been played for a fool." Thomas snarled the accusation, then darted toward him, tossing a chair out of the way before slamming his sword against Laurent's. I flinched at the sound, praying it would draw the attention of the soldiers outside. They had to know Laurent was in here, didn't they?

Laurent lunged to the side. Thomas dove toward him once more, but Laurent's feet were too light for him to be caught off-balance. They'd both had plenty of practice in the past few months it seemed, and I flinched each time metal hit metal—and even more when several figures in Iraelan red burst through the back door. Thomas gave them the briefest glance, then thrust at Laurent once more, with a furious scream that time.

I held my breath. Part of me wanted to plunge right into the middle of it, but Laurent was holding his own, and the soldiers, after a moment's hesitation, moved in on both. Thomas turned his head at the sound, then twisted back toward Laurent a second too late—one well-placed slice on his upper arm and he stumbled backward. It wasn't a fatal injury, but the chair in his way took him down as surely as a stab to the lungs.

Laurent wiped the sweat on his forehead and approached Thomas, his blade landing on his chest. "Fool," he said calmly, waving away Marius's soldiers. "Whatever will they say about you once you're gone? Think of how they'll mock you—that you died after falling over a chair."

Tears filled my eyes. Relief or fear or some misplaced sadness or long-ago loyalty,

I couldn't tell. All I knew was that I didn't want to see Thomas die. After everything . . . I still couldn't watch his life leave him.

Laurent must have sensed my emotion, for he looked toward me with a certain resignation. "Are you going to plead for his life again?" he asked. "Beg me to spare him?"

"I will not, sire." I shook my head, and the tears fell harder at the unexpected mercy—if that was in fact what it was. "Not this time."

Laurent's stance grew unyielding, his shoulders square and firm. The tip of his sword slid from Thomas's heart to his stomach, and there it stopped. I put my hand over my mouth and looked away. A painful, slow death it would be, and I was so tired of death.

"She may have decided that you are no longer worthy of mercy," Laurent said, "and I would never blame her for that decision. Your crimes against her are a thousandfold more than the ones you have committed against me." He forced a swallow, after giving me the briefest of looks. "But I will not become what Damir was. I will not cause more violence hoping to end it."

I gaped at him. All this, and Laurent was still willing to show him mercy?

"Fool?" Thomas asked. He twitched, lying there on his back. "You dare call *me* a fool?" His hand twitched toward his side, bringing out a dagger I hadn't seen before. "You have no idea—"

Laurent's blade pierced his stomach before the scream left my mouth.

CHAPTER EIGHTEEN

THE CARRIAGE JOLTED ONCE MORE AS WE HIT another rock. Wedged between Laurent and the door, I scarcely shifted on the velvet seat, but my joints were aching more with each hour that passed.

Laurent reached for my hand. "We'll stop soon."

"It's still three days back to Lochfeld, though."

I let his fingers drift over mine, though I wasn't as blasé about the remainder of the trip as he seemed to be. I'd thought riding a horse was painful, and perhaps it was, but it wasn't nearly as bad as riding in a carriage like this. I'd only been on a trip this long once before, on the way to Iraela, and those roads had been smoother.

"Yes, three days." His mouth met my ear. "And you can't leave me this time."

"Laurent!" I didn't quite swat him away, but as one of the soldiers escorting us came into the view out the window, he backed off himself. "I would never, anyway. That carriage ride with that man—it was one of the worst experiences of my life. I much prefer my husband beside me."

He did kiss me that time, and I sank against him, all soreness forgotten. Much as he might believe otherwise, I hadn't lied in the least—and the comfort he now provided, though a surprise, was more than welcome. His fingers stroked my cheek, and I closed my eyes, willing away the roughness of the road.

"Well, I prefer you here as well." His gaze grew deeper. "I meant what I said, you know —in the inn. When we return to Lochfeld, the crown will be yours."

A single tear welled up, and I brushed it away. Today was not the day for such feelings.

"I know," I replied. "The magic of the map knew, too. But I would stay beside you without it, though."

"Oh, Riette." He laughed, and the spell of the moment was broken. "You really haven't learned."

My own laugh burst out in return. Perhaps I hadn't—or perhaps I had. It was difficult to catch my breath, so long had it been since I'd laughed like this. A strange scent drifted through the carriage as I inhaled, and I sat upright, his wit forgotten.

"Laurent, that smells like—"

He interrupted me with a whistle, and the horses came to a stop atop a rolling hill. To the south was undulating farmland, soft and green, with all the trappings of spring in southern Meirdre. In the distance lay a small town I didn't know the name of—it didn't seem important enough to be placed on the map.

I pressed myself against the window as Laurent hopped down from the opposite side of the carriage. Exiting by myself would be improper, and I was learning . . . but patience was another matter. Soon enough though, he opened the door himself and helped me down.

"There's something you need to see," he said cautiously, guiding me off the dirt road and into the grass.

My slippers sank into the supple dirt, and I clung to his arm, pretending soldiers weren't surrounding us. Protection they might be, but after Vassian, I had little desire to pay them much attention. Laurent led us around the front of the carriage, and then I saw it—

Haystacks.

Haystacks in flames.

My heart threatened to leap into my throat, and I gripped his arm. Because down the hill, tossing flaming torches onto an entire field's worth of hay—an entire season's work for that farmer—were soldiers in blue Meirdrean uniforms. A single figure in brown stood to the side, likely the farmer, and my cheeks grew hot in the sun as he began to pace.

Thomas had been right. He'd told me the soldiers had burned the hay.

Soldiers burned them. Soon as they were stacked. Starve the people and their livestock and they can't rebel.

My throat grew tight. I looked up at Laurent. After all this, he'd stopped to let me witness . . . what? It didn't make any sense that he'd let me watch atrocities as they happened, did it? Not after what we'd been through. I squeezed his arm though I backed away, a question and promise at the same time.

"They're helping to destroy the stem rot," he answered quietly. "Did you really think otherwise?"

"I—" I couldn't admit that I had, not now. Nevertheless, by the way his face fell, I could tell he knew my suspicions. "I am sorry, sire."

"Apology accepted." He didn't make a move toward me. "It had to be done, my dear. The rebels spread the fungus too far and wide, and it must be stopped."

"But at what cost?" Too agitated to rein myself in, I took a step away. "You know they can't afford to replace it!"

"We certainly can't let it spread between farms." He sighed. "That's a hay merchant down there. If he had sold it, it might have reached throughout the entire region. He's been compensated for the hay, as well as for the work he did last season that was all for naught."

"But—you compensated him? You order the soldiers here?"

"Guilty." Laurent lifted a shoulder. "An entire squad—led by Captain Erstad—is crossing the kingdom, carrying coin and burning what needs to be burned. It was the least I could do. And lest you think you had no part in those . . . it was all due to you."

I blew out a breath and stepped close to him once more. "I'm sorry I doubted you."

"I don't blame you. I could never blame you for that. Wish that things had been otherwise from the start, yes, that I do."

I looked up at him, and his eyes were dark, even though the sun was still hanging above the horizon. He had hurt me, and I had hurt him, but somehow, we'd survived it all. And the future? It drew me toward it like the map in Lochfeld did, and the idea of it had ceased to be frightening.

"I think I'd like to watch a bit longer, if you don't mind," I said. "It's beautiful, in an odd way."

Laurent pulled me close, and I leaned my head on his shoulder.

"For as long as you want," he replied.

And so we stood there on top of that hill, arm in arm, as the sun set and embers danced into the sky.

EPILOGUE

LAURENT

THE SMILE ON RIETTE'S FACE FLICKERED unevenly as Laurent knelt before her in the throne room at Lochfeld. Whether she was thinking of the apple blossoms in the orchard outside or the hundred pairs of eyes on her, he didn't know, and he didn't care. She had agreed to this ceremony, and that meant more than he had words for. He would have avoided it of course, had she wished it, but agreeing meant so much.

He smiled at her, perched uncomfortably on her throne, and her eyes grew solemn with duty and love as he knelt before her. She stretched out her hand without his prompting, and he kissed the back of it, wishing he could kiss so much more of her. He contained himself though and reached for the crown on the small table next to him. Riette's lips parted as he stood and placed the crown on her head, and his heart skipped a beat. Had it hurt her again?

But she gave him the slightest nod, the agreed upon sign that the magic was cooperating, at least for tonight. Like a wave, it was, retreating and advancing—at least, that was how she'd tried to describe it. He doubted he could ever fully understand the gift she'd been blessed with, and maybe that was for the best. The guilt would fill him forever . . . already did, to some extent. He didn't deserve her, not the crownkeeper, not the wife.

Giving her one last bow, he helped her to her feet and watched her waver on unsteady feet before catching herself and smiling at him. Laurent could tell she was pretending the applauding crowd didn't exist, and that was just fine with him, too. He would never complain that she was focused on him and no one else.

"We walked like this once before," she whispered as he took her hand, and they strode toward the doors at the back of the throne room. "Do you remember?"

Laurent raised her hand to his mouth and kissed it again, a violation of protocol that he couldn't bring himself to care about. What would his courtiers do? Talk? They'd been doing that for years, and now that rumors of the *occurrence* in Windersay had almost certainly reached Meirdre, he doubted Riette's part in it was much of a secret any longer.

"I remember how nervous you were to dance with me," he replied. "And how much I wanted an excuse to put my hands on you."

"I was." Her cheeks flushed, and he looked away for an instant to gather emotions more proper for a public event. "And I suspected as much of you."

"And now?"

She lowered her voice even further. "I wish all these people would go away so we could dance all night without having to stop for politeness's sake."

His smile split his face, even though it wasn't dancing that first was on his mind. As a consolation prize, yes, it was that. "Duty first, my darling." His mouth met her ear. "But I suspect we can still fit some dancing in. Who am I to deny you what you want on a night like this? But first—"

Her nose wrinkled. "But first what?"

"Captain Erstad!" he called. Riette's eyes widened as the captain approached, and Laurent both loved and hated what he was about to do. "I believe my wife has something she'd like to say to you."

Riette glanced backward, as though escape was possible, then forced a smile. "Captain. It's so very nice to see you again. Are you enjoying the evening?"

"I am, Your Majesty." Erstad forced his own smile. "Especially at Lochfeld."

Laurent squeezed her hand. He'd already reprimanded Erstad for losing her, but part of that accountability fell to her as well.

"About that—" Her smile became more natural. "I am sorry about the position I put you in. I was reckless and foolish and not becoming of one chosen to lead Lochfeld in the king's place. I should have trusted you."

"Never mind that." He cocked his head to the side. "It was a learning experience—enemy armies, I can handle, but queens are something altogether different, I have learned. And for my part, I am sorry I failed you. If will not happen again, Your Majesty."

"Then we are even?" Riette asked. "For now?" she added with a glint in her eyes.

"We are indeed." Erstad gave her a short

bow before disappearing once more—for more wine, Laurent was certain.

"Your Majesties!" The crowd gathering in the ballroom parted as Juliana scurried toward them. His sister curtsied before taking Riette's hands in hers and kissing each of her cheeks. "I'm so happy for you."

Riette brushed her palms over her skirt, a heavy gold velvet embroidered with red silk. "King Marius," she replied, "returned some of your mother's dowry. A fraction of it went to the dress. The rest—"

"Yes, yes." Juliana tossed her hair. "To the treasury, to allow my dear brother to suspend taxes for five years. I wonder who could have possibly convinced him to do that?"

"At least you used your time in Iraela wisely," Laurent cut in, "though I suspect I'll be hearing about how you convinced Marius to return the dowry money for much longer than those five years."

It was a polite lie. He didn't only suspect —he knew, because he knew Juliana. But if that was what it had taken to solidify the union with Marius and gain some of his own coin back, he would consider it an even exchange and then some.

"Perhaps." Juliana grinned at him, then curtsied again and vanished into the crowd.

Laurent brushed his fingers against Riette's, an apology and promise. The musicians departed, but he scarcely noticed. And once the courtiers drifted out of the ballroom, Juliana and her husband disappeared to whatever room upstairs they'd appropriated this time, and the map became visible under his feet, he wound a hand around Riette's waist and drew her against him.

"You can see the map now," he said, tugging her backward into a casual waltz. "Not so many feet."

"I could see it before." She leaned her head on his shoulder and closed her eyes, as though the power of the place was overwhelming. "It made sure of that."

"Does it ever leave you alone?" His fingers alighted on her hair.

"Well—" Riette missed a step, and he gripped her hand while she caught her balance. "Yes. Most of the time, at least. But it seems to know I'm here now, and it's leaving me alone for the most part—though it's letting me know that there's so much more I need to learn."

"Father Gerritt will help you with that." The priest had cornered him earlier that morning and all but ordered him to send Riette to his library every day next week to pore over whatever texts he could find. "Though something tells me you know more than you think."

"I'm learning. But I'm afraid I'm not very good at interpreting the magic yet—and using it is something completely different. Maybe I'll never figure it out. The water—I scarcely knew what I was doing in Winder-say. Even worse, the sword." Her voice grew quiet. "I'm afraid of letting the map work through me like that again."

"Hmm." He let his lips drift down her jawline as he hummed a folk song, a traditional Elternow melody. "Somehow I think you will learn."

"Laurent!" Riette pulled away, her eyes wide with delight. "Where did you learn that?"

"Your parents," he admitted. They'd appeared at Lochfeld last week when summoned, then fled back to Elternow immediately after. Their new farm needed managing, they'd claimed, and Laurent had let them go, realizing that accepting their daughter as their new queen wouldn't be an immediate happening. "Though I wasn't able to convince them to attend tonight, I convinced your mother to teach me the melody."

"I wouldn't imagine even you could convince them to celebrate a coronation. The very idea would intimidate anyone from Elternow—including me." Her face fell for a fraction of a second, but then she recovered. "I will pay them a visit as soon as the farm work allows, and until then, I will satisfy myself with you."

"Shameless." He drew her against him once more. "And yet I shall do the same."

Riette closed her eyes and laid her head against his chest. He hummed the rest of the melody as he led her around the ballroom, over the map that would protect Meirdre for the rest of his reign.

All thanks to her.

ACKNOWLEDGMENTS

Writing a trilogy is something I hadn't done until I realized Riette's story hadn't ended with *Treason's Crown*—and writing the last book in a trilogy is more complicated than I'd expected, as it turns out. Thanks to the readers who cheered me on, Meghan, who read the entire thing and gasped in the appropriate places, and Cathy, who found all those embarrassing missing words in my sentences. I'm so grateful for your support in closing in out this series.

ABOUT THE AUTHOR

Anne Wheeler grew up with her nose in a book but earned two degrees in aviation before it occurred to her she was allowed to write her own. When not working, moving, or writing her next novel, she can be found planning her next escape to the desert—camera gear included. She currently lives in Georgia with her husband, son, and herd of cats.

For more information:
www.anne-wheeler.com